The Stories Grandma Forgot

(and How I Found Them)

The Stories Grandma Forgot

(and How I Found Them)

Nadine Aisha Jassat
Illustrated by Sandhya Prabhat

Orion

ORION CHILDREN'S BOOKS

First published in Great Britain in 2023
by Hodder & Stoughton

3 5 7 9 10 8 6 4 2

Text copyright © Nadine Aisha Jassat, 2023
Illustrations copyright © Sandhya Prabhat, 2023

The moral rights of the author and illustrator have been asserted.

A CIP catalogue record for this book
is available from the British Library.

ISBN 978 1 510 11157 8

Typeset in Trebuchet
Printed and bound in Great Britain by Clays Ltd, Elcograf S.p.A.

The paper and board used in this book
are made from wood from responsible sources.

Orion Children's Books
An imprint of
Hachette Children's Group
Part of Hodder & Stoughton
Carmelite House
50 Victoria Embankment
London EC4Y 0DZ

An Hachette UK Company
www.hachette.co.uk

www.hachettechildrens.co.uk

For my time-traveller

A NOTEBOOK FULL OF QUESTIONS

I AM

Today in English,
the teacher asked us to write
about who we are.

I could see my friend Jess
scribbling next to me,
her pen moving fast across the page.

I looked up at the prompt on the board,
the words 'I Am' standing out like a challenge,
like they're asking for something more
than I really understand.

I am   called Nyla Elachi.
       or NNN-EYYYE-LA to people I meet for the first time,
       or NYLA, NYLA, PANTS ON FIRE to a certain bully
       who I swear won't make me cry.
       I'm Sweetie to my grandma, and Sweet Pea to my mum.
       Both of them sound like: *mine*.

I am   a girl who helps look after her grandmother,
       and her memory-magic brain.
       My dad died when I was four.
       I don't know what he would have called me.
       Sweetie? Daughter? Nyla?

I am   the words 'It's going to be okay,'
       that I whisper to myself,
       whenever I feel afraid.
       I wear the same school jumper every day.
       It's way too big for me, but Mum says
       I've got to grow into its sleeves
       (even though they've already started to fray).

I am   the person who gets asked big questions,
        like *Where Are You From?* straight away,
        before someone has got to know me,
        their words trying to put me in a box, or a cage.

I am   the quiet voice that whispers,
        (even though I want to say: *None of your business*)
        after people have guessed a million countries
        that they think match my face:
        I'm mixed. My mum is white,
        and though people always think
        we don't look alike,
        I think it's because they're not looking right:
        they're not seeing what I see.
        My dad and grandma are from Zimbabwe,
        and their mix is Brown and Black,
        their mix is full of stories,
        stories that I wish I had,
        ever since my dad passed.
        Stories that are part of me.

I am   a girl who makes promises to everyone else,
        but if I was to make one to myself,
        it would be this:

        to have the words, one day,
        to say exactly what I mean.
        To know how to answer the question:
        'I Am'.

PART 1

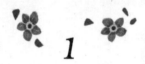

1

LIFE IS LIKE THE BUSES

MY MORNING

My morning started with the crunch of toast between teeth:
Mum + Grandma + Me.

It moved with our own flow:
Mum grabbed Grandma's red coat,
and I reminded Grandma how to put on her shoes,
as she leaned down and whispered:
'Time for dancing, Sweetie!'

'Hello, dear!' Grandma shout-waved
as she climbed into the day-care bus,
to a lady walking past.
'You're looking lovely today!'

Followed by the noise of a zip closing,
as Mum sneaked a note into my bag:

And her stifled yawn,
after working back-to-back shifts,
in an office during the day,
and cleaning at night.
She's just one person trying to earn enough
to stretch over the three of us.

Then walking to school as fast as I can —
until I see a figure skulking towards me,
slowly filling me with dread:

'What're you looking at, Elachi?'

A BRIEF HISTORY OF HARRY

Harry is in the year above,
and for reasons
I can't understand,
he always seems to
single me
out
and make me
feel
on edge.
I've seen him do it to other people,
but not as much as me.

My friend Jess said,
that on a swimming trip in Juniors,
he stole someone's clothes,
and threw them in the pool.

Jess said that person now goes to another school.

I don't want that to happen to me.
I keep my head down,
hoping he'll leave me alone eventually —

but
        he never does.

WORDS IN THE MUD

When Harry's blue eyes look me up and down,
my reply falls out of my mouth,
and gets lost in the mud by my feet.

'Aren't you gonna answer me?
What. Are. You. Looking.
AT!'

Harry lunges,
his white hands spread out wide,
then laughs
as if he can see how
my tummy flips
uʍop ǝpᴉsdn
and inside out,
as I start to feel smaller
and smaller
and less
and less like me,
until I see the smile up ahead of me
of the friendliest face
who pushes past Harry,
multicoloured bobbles bouncing in her light-brown hair,
linking her arm through mine:

'What's up, Elachi?'

'Hey, Jess.'

ALL ABOUT JESS

I've known Jess since first year,
when *everyone* was new to school,
but I was new to *here*.

The teacher asked us to introduce ourselves
to the person sitting next to us.
I didn't know what to say,
so, I tried: 'I've just moved from the other side of town.'

'Really?' Jess exclaimed enthusiastically,
freckles dancing across her cheeks.
'Tell. Me. *Everything*.'

Everything felt huge,
but I did my best:
I told her about me,
and Mum and Grandma.
After, she asked more and more:

'Would you rather own a chihuahua or a husky?'
'Are you a Gemini? Cancer? Libra? I KNEW IT!'
'We can have lunch together, if you want?'

That was over 365 lunches ago.
We've been friends ever since.

MISSING MARSHMALLOWS

It wasn't long before I opened up to Jess about Dad.

Lying on her bedroom floor,
doing homework for maths,
we were learning about fractions,
and had just been delivered hot chocolate by her dad,
with marshmallows balanced like fluffy clouds on top.

When I told her about my dad,
she listened.
'I wish I had more memories of him,' I said,
not adding how I wish
he would bring me hot chocolate
with his own custom topping,
or ask me about school.

Jess looked down at the checked lines
and scribbles on her workbook page.
'Maybe ... he's not gone completely,
in all the things that are left of him,'
she whispered,
before turning to me with the biggest smile,
'Like you! And you're super cool.'

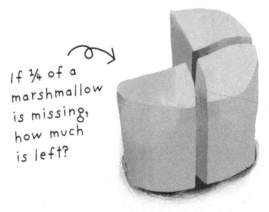

If ¼ of a
marshmallow
is missing,
how much
is left?

9

And then we slurped our hot chocolates,
giggling as whipped cream tickled our noses.

If I'm what's left of Dad,
then Grandma is too —
she's his mum
(and my best friend).

What's left of him are the lines
around Mum's eyes and cheeks,
the ones from all the times he made her laugh
(and the ones from after he died).

And all of my questions,
that I wish I could ask him.
All the missing stories —
the sound of Mum's silence,
when I want to know more.

What's left of him are
Grandma's memories:
twinkling lights in the dark.
Memories which are
like shooting stars

slowly
fading
away.

ALZHEIMER'S (NOUN)

When Mum first told me
what Grandma's forgetting was called —
Alzheimer's —
I thought about how it sounded
like it had a
'*Hi*' in the middle
even though it feels like
the opposite, like
the person is slowly walking away.

Mum says to think of it like time-travel:
like Grandma's mind is journeying
to another time or place.
I see Grandma time-travel
when she calls me
>   *Nurse?*
>
>   Or   *Girl?*
>
>   Or   *Honey?*

I try and remind her:
'Look, Grandma, it's me,
Sweetie!'

A name I love.
A name that feels so good to call my own.

But when she looks at me it's like
she's

>   not

>   really

>   here.

When she looks at me
it's like she's living somewhere else,
and I'm the one far away,
reaching for those two letters:
'Hi'.
A word that I understand
in a bigger word that I really don't:
Alzheimer's.

FORM PERIOD

When Mr Davis calls my name,
I think about how it's the third time today
that I've heard 'Elachi',
but how each time it's felt different.

In Harry's mouth it feels hard,
like he's taken something precious to me,
and twisted it, tainted it.

In Jess's it feels like part of this whirlwind
of her, of all her different energetic words.
I know that if I looked in the Jess Dictionary,
Elachi would be listed under *friend*.

And from Mr Davis, it feels all 2D,
like it's missing its history,
its story.

STORIES LIKE ELACHI SEEDS

Recently, on a good day,
Grandma split open a cardamom pod,
and held it up to my nose.

'Elachi,' she said, pointing at the open line
running down the small seed pod.
'Elachi also means cardamom.'

We leaned down together,
and sniffed, the rich smell
filling our noses.

'Remember,' Grandma said,
and held me close.
'Elachi. It's my name.
The one I passed on to your dad,
and you. The one I'll never change.'

That's what my name means to me.
It means Grandma, and family.
It means stories, tucked up inside Grandma
like elachi seeds,
like the gold in a cardamom pod.

'NYLA, ARE YOU LISTENING TO ME?'

Mr Davis's frown is a semi-circle
as I look up from my desk.
Everyone else
has started filing out of class,
but Mr Davis is standing over me:
'You were almost late again this morning.
You do remember what we spoke about
with your mum last term?'

Behind him, Jess wriggles her eyebrows,
making them jump up and down
as she heads out of the door.

'I remember, Mr Davis,' I say,
and I do: my grades making that small dip,
from *very good* to *just okay*.

'This term is a chance for a fresh start —
you're a good student, and your friend Jessica, too.
I want to see you really apply yourself,
and pull those grades back up.'
Mr Davis gestures with his hands
in a way that makes me picture my grades like socks
being pulled up to the knees.

Nerves squirm inside me as I nod vigorously.
'Yes, Mr Davis.'

'Good. I look forward to hearing excellent
reports by the end of term.
Mr Harkin's history project is coming up,'
he says, as he turns
and makes his way back to his desk,
'perhaps you can start there.'
He looks at me meaningfully:
'Remember, Nyla, less lateness,
more greatness!'

I wonder what novelty mug
he got that slogan from.

LIFE IS LIKE THE BUSES

I remember reading a cheesy slogan
on Mr Davis's mug over and over at parents' evening last term,
while he spoke to Mum and Grandma.

After Mr Davis told Mum about my grades,
I couldn't stop her from wanting to sit down with me,
exhausted after work,
to ask about my homework.

'I'm just trying to help,' she'd say,
until I insisted that I didn't need it,
with Grandma piping up:
'She's got her Sweetie Smarts!'

'Are you sure you don't need my help, Sweet Pea?'
Mum would ask.
'I know how much you do for Grandma
too, and if it's too much—'

'No! My grades are going to be great next term,
you'll see.'

I remember when Mr Davis said
I'd been late to registration once —
and how the school was aiming
'for a maximum attendance policy' —
how Mum's voice changed,
her Yorkshire accent standing strong
like it does every time she stands up for me:
'Nyla's *never* been late to a lesson,' she pointed out.

I remember how Grandma leaned forward, and said
with a classic Grandma grin:
'Life is like the buses, lovelies —
it runs on its own time!'

What I know most of all
is how time with Grandma is better
than anything else —
how she makes everything
feel okay,
in her magic, marvellous,
Grandma way.

She *even* made Mr Davis laugh.

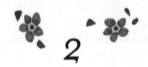

2

THE GIFT OF FLIGHT

MY TIME

Every day,
on my walk home from school —
between the bell ringing at 3.15
and the day-care bus dropping off Grandma at 4.30 —
I visit a special space
where you can find people's words
from hundreds of years ago,
and others fresh, hot off the press,
all kept in the sandy brick building
hidden between a row of trees,
and a newsagent's across the road:
the library.

Before Dad died,
we rented a house in the town
where he and Mum grew up.
We've moved a lot since then:
each time the places get smaller and smaller,
and the landlords meaner and meaner,
and Grandma vaguer and vaguer.

But we've been this side of town for ages now.
The library was the first place I discovered
and I've been coming ever since.

When I walk through the heavy wooden doors,
the quiet wraps round me
as I pass the curves of the front desk,
heading towards bookshelves so familiar
they feel like my own.

It feels like walking into a sanctuary.
A space where nothing's being asked of me.
No Harry. No Mr Davis. No planning ahead.
No worry about Grandma. Or questions about Dad.
Here I can just sink my head into a book,
and read.

BUT, TODAY

There's a boy sitting in my usual place,
bent over a book,
bum plonked on my lime-green bean bag of choice,
hiding his face as he turns a page.

I stop still,
and he looks up,
then around,
as if to check if it's him I'm staring at.

He looks at me,
large blue round glasses slightly
too big for his face,
as he says,

'Erm, hi?'

WHAT I WANT TO SAY

I want to say   'That book you're holding is the second in the
                   series so don't start there.'
I want to say   'I hardly ever see other kids my age in here.'
I want to say   'If you want any recommendations I've got loads,
                   I've read most of them twice!'
I want to say   'Hi.'

WHAT I ACTUALLY SAY

'Er, yeah, hi, sorry,' I mutter,
'I'm not used to seeing anyone else here.'
I move to look at the New In display.

The boy leans forward,
wobbling slightly on the bean bag
as he adjusts his position.

'It's my first time,' he says.
'I usually swim after school,
but I hurt my wrist.'
He holds up a brown hand,
wrapped in a peach cast.
'Mum said I needed to find something
to occupy me while it heals.'

I look at him from behind the pages of a hardback book.
'How did you hurt it?'

'I was hanging out at my uncle's place.'
He pushes his glasses up as he explains:
'Well, my great-uncle, technically,
but you know how it is.'

I wonder, for a beat, if I do —
but it means so much that he thinks I might,
that I keep that wondering to myself,
and don't say anything.

'Anyway, he said not to move a box,
but I wanted to help, and then,
as I was going up the stairs,
I slipped trying to balance it
and—'

He holds up his hands like a magician:

'Here I am!'

His laugh is small,
but light.

'What did your gre— your uncle say?'
I ask.

His laugh is bigger this time.

'He's pretty chill. He said' —
and the boy's voice changes,
fills with a Jamaican accent,
deep with warmth:

*'Raymond, you may not be blessed with the gift
of balance, but for a moment there
coming down them stairs,
I thought you had the gift of flight!'*

I imagine the boy, Raymond, mid-air,
and I can't help my laugh —
but then I cover my mouth
and wince as I picture his landing.

'It's okay,' he says, noticing my expression change.
He waves the book with his injured hand,
as if to illustrate. 'It's just sprained.
But you know what parents are like:
my mum's banned me from anything
that doesn't involve sitting down.'

I don't really know what parents (plural)
are like, but I nod, anyway.

He's shared something of him,
and now it's my turn,
that's how making friends works.
But something in my chest feels too heavy
to think about parents,
and people who have great-uncles
who laugh at their mistakes,
to stay.

'It was nice to meet you,
Raymond,' I say.

His mouth forms a small '*o*':
'It's just Ray!'

He looks sad that I'm leaving,

So, before I go,
I tell Ray my name.

'I'm Nyla, by the way.'

Ray smiles,
and suddenly his glasses
are the exact right size for his face.

'Nice to meet you back, Nyla,' he says.

BEEP

I try to scan my book in the library machine
but it says:
'Error: Not in Use.'
I try again, bending the book a different way,
my cheeks warming as I hope Ray doesn't see.

Beep. Beep.
Error, again.

Behind me, I hear a gentle cough,
and turn to see the librarian waving,
from behind the desk.

'Sorry, the machines aren't working,' she says.
'I can scan that out for you, if you like?'

She's not the *usual* librarian —
Ms Bow has red hair and a grumpy manner
that I kinda like, as she leaves me to do my thing.
But this new librarian looks so familiar
as I walk closer; I just can't quite place her face.

'Nice to see you again,' she says.

I stare.
Have we met before?

'What?' I ask, really hoping now
that those aren't Ray's eyes
I can feel staring into my back,
as I try to play it cool.

'This morning, sorry, you don't remember me —
I walk past your house on my way to work —
your grandma was waving?'

My face is some combination of
blank
and
who?

'She said I was looking lovely, I think?
A very nice way to start my morning!'
It's like the librarian's face rearranges,
a jigsaw puzzle of hesitant smile and long dark hair,
and in my memory the picture is suddenly clear:
the woman Grandma accosted
on her way on to the bus this morning.

'It was you!'

The librarian laughs.

'It was! I live just down the road from you.
Sometimes I see your grandma in the window
when I'm on my way to work.
She always waves at me.'

Huh. This is new.

'She remembers you?'

The librarian smiles.

'Of course, she's my window waver!'
She slides my book, freshly scanned,
back over. 'Say hi to your grandma for me,'
she says.

The library is full of surprises today.

3

A ROOM TO DREAM IN

LATE, AGAIN

I'm racing home to be in
for when day care
drops Grandma off.
The book in my backpack
hits against me as I run:
thum-thum-thum.

Grandma climbs off the bus,
smiling in her little red coat,
and waving to the other passengers
as if she is royalty.

I am breathless,
but I am there.

Grandma's carer walks her up to the gate.
Her name is Maria,
and she has blonde hair
that she once dyed green.
Grandma used to look at it,
frown, and say:
'Seaweed.'
I'd try not to laugh.

'Is your mum in, Nyla?' Maria asks.

'Yes! She's just making our tea,'
and my big smile
hides the lie.
Maria nods,
ushering Grandma
— who gives a last regal wave
to the folks on the bus —
towards me.

I'm never sure if Maria believes me,
but as long as I've said it,
we can both pretend
it's true.

The truth is: Mum hasn't been able to be home
for Grandma's day-care drop-off in ages.

The truth is: we need Mum to work this much
to pay Grandma's care fees,
and everything else,
because it's a lot.

The truth is: Grandma's my best friend.
And I can do this.
I'm twelve years old.
It's enough.

AFTER-SCHOOL CHAT

Grandma's smile is warm when she sees me:
'*There* you are, Sweetie.'

It makes me feel like she missed me.

'Here I am, Grandma,' I say.
'How was your day?'

'Oh, we toodled and we tweedled.
Sweetie, we danced ourselves inside out!
It was the best night of my life!'

'Okay, Grandma,' I say with a laugh,
walking her back inside.
'Well, my day was so-so,
I had a run-in with Mr Davis,
you know the one.'

Grandma makes a raspberry face,
blowing hard.

'Exactly.' I laugh again.
'But then, I also maybe
made a new friend,
and I met a friend of yours,
the lady who works at the library.
She said you wave at her through the window?'

Grandma looks away, then back at me.
'There's a whole world out there,'
she says.

I smile. 'There is.'
And even when she feels far away,
I know Grandma is adventuring in it.

THE THINGS GRANDMA FORGOT
(AND HOW I FOUND THEM)

It started small at first:
hanging up the telephone,
but forgetting who she'd spoken to
(so, I called them back on redial,
and figured it all out).

Then making cups of tea,
and leaving them
all over the house
(so, I collected each one,
and made her something fresh).

Then sometimes
she'd put things together
like she'd forgotten what was what:
sandwiches filled with washing-up liquid,
or a summer dress with winter socks.

But through it all she was still Grandma,
still telling me stories about Zimbabwe,
and always knowing who I was.
Always knowing the story of us.

But now when I ask:

'Grandma, what was it like
when you first moved to the UK?'

Her answers become vaguer and vaguer:

'A dooo be dee dap
dap dap dap!

A doo be dee dap dap doo!

'Grandma, what was Dad like
when he was my age?'

'Age is just a number, Sweetie,
it's what's in the heart that counts!'

I know there's a story in there,
in all of Grandma's sayings and songs,
but I'm not sure how to find it,
in between the mix of what she has
and hasn't forgotten.

I think she knows it too,
the way sometimes she goes quiet,
and says to me:
'Sweetie — there's something,
there's someone ...'
and I wish I had a time-travel-translator,
to help her get her words,
so she can tell me what I need to find for her.

I need Grandma's stories,
to help understand who I am —
to help understand my dad.
But how can I do that
when they're fading away
with every washing-up liquid sandwich,
and question mark at the end of my name:
'Sweetie?'

'I'm here, Grandma,'
I always say.
And that will never change.

A ROOM TO DREAM IN

Grandma and I settle down in front of the TV.
Grandma sits in her cosy chair by the window,
and I prop myself up on the faded sofa opposite.
Our living room is small enough
that we can reach out and touch hands —
that we're never far apart.

We don't watch TV as much as we used to.
Mum says the electricity bill keeps going up and up,
but when I ask her about it,
she says that it makes her happy when she's at work
to think of me and Grandma all curled up,
watching one of those holiday home shows.

'It's important to have some room to dream,'
she says.

Some days we watch the quiz shows,
sometimes Grandma dozes off
in the middle of an afternoon movie,
usually a mystery,
where I always try to guess whodunnit.

When today's show ends,
I get up to switch the TV off,
the room filled with Grandma's sleeping hum.
I hear a voice on the gravel outside.
I creep close to the curtain,
undertaking my own investigation.
Mum stands outside,
her back to the window,
phone pressed against her ear.

'Thank you, Maria.
I know Farida really enjoys her visits with you.
Mmmhmm, sorry I didn't catch you.
Yes, Nyla was right, I was just busy cooking.
You know how it is.'
(That's Mum's thinking-on-her-feet
Mmmhmm,
with a touch of her please-let-this-be-over-with
Mmmmhmmm).

Mum goes quiet for a while,
and I almost think she has hung up
but I can still see the phone lighting her face,
her mouth pinched and her eyes tired.

'I'll look into it,' she says,
'I'll find some time —
leave it with me, okay?'

After Mum hangs up,
she stands outside.
I feel like I'm watching something I shouldn't be:
the way after her face goes from a smile,
to hanging so low,
it's like gravity pulled her to the floor.

I've never seen her like this.

THE PROMISE

Grandma has always lived with us,
even when Dad was alive.
Mum says she made a promise to Dad
that she'd look out for his family
as if they were her own.
After he died, she made that promise to Grandma:
that she wouldn't be alone.

Once, Jess asked Mum
if Grandma was going to move into a care home,
and I kicked her under the table.

'No,' Mum said. 'We're going to keep her
at home with us as long as we can.'
When Jess asked why,
Mum said: 'I promised.'

'What promise?' Jess had said,
and Mum just looked at her,
and walked out of the room.

I worried what Jess would think,
but she'd just turned to me and said:
'Your mum is so cool.'

I think what Jess misses in subtlety,
she makes up for in a big imagination.

Later, Jess said that she thinks
my mum wants to keep Grandma close
because she's a part of my dad.

But it's not just that —
Mum *never* talks about him.
And, she has me.

I think what Jess doesn't understand
is the thing I love about my mum the most —
the one thing I get from her, too —
when we make a promise to someone,
we keep it. And that's what Mum
is trying to do.

SHOE GROOVES

When Mum finally comes in and sits down
she makes an 'ooomph' noise,
like every breath
that has been propping her up
has now been let out.

She takes off her shoes,
her feet marked with indentations
from where they push in on her every day,
walking to and from the bus stop,
and up and down at work.

Mum asks me about school,
while her eyes look over Grandma's dozing face —
the evening is when Grandma's memory fades the most,
as if it goes down at the same time as the sun.

I think about telling Mum about Mr Davis,
how I'm going to do really well this term,
but I don't want to remind her of my grades.
I think about telling her about meeting Ray,
but then I feel shy —
what if I don't see him again,
what if it's too soon to say
I've made a new friend.

So instead,
I throw myself on to the sofa next to Mum,
and tell her about the new librarian
who waves at Grandma.

Mum's face smiles as she listens,
but all I see
is the way her hands rub
at the indentations on her feet.

BEDTIME

Mum gets called into work —
a last-minute cleaning shift, double time.

I take Grandma to bed,
holding her small hand as we climb up the stairs,
then passing her toothbrush,
'It's time to do your teeth!'
as she looks at me, her eyes soft and watery.

'There, there,' I say,
when she spits out the toothpaste,
and I pass her my sparkly mermaid cup,
to swill her mouth with water.

'Thank you,' is her small reply.

'There, there,' I say,
as I remind her to put her nightie on.

'Thank you,' is her small reply.

'There, there,' I say,
when she's all tucked up in bed.
'Grandma, you're just like a bedbug tonight,
all cosy and wrapped up in your blanket burrito!'

'Thank you,' is her reply.

At the corner of her mouth is a small smile,
and though I can't tell if she's fully in this time,
she turns her face to me,
and we stare at each other
in the sliver of moonlight.

I want to say *I miss you*
as she looks into my eyes,
but I don't.

I just hold her gaze,
as her hand brushes my face.

'There, there,' she says to me,
her touch sure and soft,
just like it has always been.

'Thank you,' is my small reply.

4

OUR MONTH OF SUNDAYS

'Dooo be dee dap
dap doo! Bah!'

I wake up slowly,
the sound of singing filling my ears.

'Doo be dee
dap dap dee!'

I open one eye,
glance around my room:
to the bumpy ceiling Mum says was decorated in the 1980s,
same pink and purple bedspread.
I close it again.

'Doooo be dee
dap dap HEY!'

I open both eyes,
and with them let in my whole world:
Grandma, standing at my door,
grinning down at me.

'Dooo de dee dap
dap dee, SWEETIE!'

she sings.

A smile creeps at the corner of my mouth.
Just as I am about to open it,
to match a tune with Grandma's,
I hear another voice join in:

'Dooo do do dooo
DOO DOO beep!'

Mum takes Grandma's hands,
singing with her,
Grandma shuffling on our landing
like a dancefloor,
in her nightie and fluffy slippers,
Mum singing into her toothbrush.

The morning light comes in through my curtains,
glinting over everything.
It reminds me of the disco ball
Jess had at her birthday party last term,
as if for a second we are in another time and place —
dancing the night away.
I smile as my feet hit the floor,
and Mum and Grandma cheer.
It's their faces that tell me what time it is
and what day.

I jump into the circle of Mum and Grandma
singing made-up songs around me,
singing the sounds
of Sunday,
joining in with a whirl:

'And a doo be dee
dap dap dee!'

NEVER IN A MONTH OF SUNDAYS

Sundays are our family day,
it's the only time Mum never works,
and we hang out just us three.

Mum's always coming out with
funny phrases, like if she thinks
something is unbelievable,
she'll say: 'Never in a month of Sundays!'

She doesn't know that I wish for that:
a month where every day,
it's me, Mum and Grandma.
It's our Sundays.

ROLLING THROUGH THE SUPERMARKET

We get the bus to the supermarket first.
It's my job to look after Grandma,
to keep her from wandering too far
in her memory-magic way,
while Mum goes through the shopping list
for the week ahead.

Right now,
Mum is in the tinned food aisle,
counting under her breath by a three-for-two.
I know she's doing money maths in her head.

That's when I notice
Grandma's not with me.

I turn on my heel
to see the corner of her red wool coat
blinking out of sight.

I dash before I can think.

Speed round one aisle —
crisps and snacks —
see Grandma
at the other end
knocking into a woman
who drops everything,
multipacks falling to the ground.

'Excuse me!' the woman shouts,
but Grandma is a dot
that keeps tottering along,
like she's taken super-speed pills
alongside her usual daily mix.

I pass the woman, want to yell:
'Clean-up on aisle six!'
But Grandma's heading out of the door now,
so instead I shout: 'Grandma!'

She doesn't turn.
Her little red coat,
dark hair in a plait,
bobbing out into the day.

I RUN TO CATCH HER UP

I know what people think.
They see me running
and they look behind me,
not at me.
Not realising I'm running towards someone,
not away.
I push away their judgements,
what Mum calls their 'p-r-e-j-u-d-i-c-e'.
I picture Grandma shaking her finger at them:
'Fools!' she'd say.
The memory keeps my focus straight:
I will get Grandma.
It will be okay.
Today is my month of Sundays.

'OOOMPH!'

is the noise I make,
    when running out of the supermarket
      at such fast a pace,
        that I run straight into a wall
          of red wool,
            stood still.

OH, GRANDMA

'Oh, Grandma.'
There are tears on her face.
I wipe her cheeks,
with the edge of my sleeve.
'Are you okay?
Come on, let's go inside
and find Mum.'

Grandma looks at me,
and I can't tell if she is here,
or if she is time-travelling.

'I saw him!' she says,
and I wipe another tear away.
'He was here!
I called to him.
I was so loud,
but he did not listen to me,
"Stop, stop!" I said,
and he just kept going.
Why didn't he stay?'

'Who, Grandma?' I ask.

Her expression is incredulous,
like she can't believe
I don't understand.

'Basim!' she says,
with a stamp of her foot,
and stops time
with a single word.

Basim.
My dad.

A WISH

I know it's probably Grandma's memory,
but I can't help it:
I look around immediately,
but it's just a jumble of people
rushing to their cars.

When I look back at Grandma,
I don't think I can face telling her
the truth — that Dad died eight years ago,
and no amount of her time-travelling
can change that.

When we find Mum, she exclaims:
'Where did you two get off to?'

I fuss Grandma away,
and don't tell Mum what happened.

I can't bear seeing the hurt
on Mum's face, too.

I wish it was easy
to sing all these problems away,
to go back to how our day started
with a

doo be dee
doop doop dah.
A doo be dee
dap dap ah.

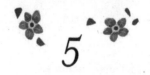

5

WORDS ARE IMPORTANT

FRIEND MEETING AT BREAK

In registration,
I lean over to Jess,
slide a note along her desk:
'Friend Meeting at Break:
Grandma update.'

She nods, tucks it under her folder,
and with a not-so-subtle straight face
pretends to stare ahead.

Two hours later,
we huddle under the awning
overlooking the school field.

'*Alors,*' Jess says, dramatically,
reminding me next period is French.
'*Qu'est-que c'est, la problème avec ta grand-mère,
aujourd'hui, ma chérie?*'
I laugh.

'*Elle est ...*'
I look around,
trying to find a way to describe it.
'You know how my grandma's been, like—'

'—a teensy tiny bit ever-so-slightly hugely forgetful?'
Jess supplies.

'Yes. Well, yesterday, in the supermarket—'

'—the big one or the little one?'

'The big, what's that got to do—?'

'I just like to picture the scene in my mind,
like a director would—'

'—okay, well, yesterday in the *big* supermarket,
Grandma ran off outside.'

'Oh no.'

'Yeah, and when I caught up with her
she was all upset, and—'

I stop, aware I sound slightly ridiculous.
'She said she'd seen my dad.'

'Oh, shiz.'

A beat, before Jess speaks again:
'Like, *seen him* seen him?
Like, there in the supermarket?
Like, for real?'

'Yeah.'

'Hmm.' Jess leans back against the wall,
then springs forward,
as if remembering the chewing gum
that's usually stuck there.
'Do you think it was just someone who looked like him?'

'I didn't see anyone. It was mainly
just families with kids and that.'

'Oh, Grandma Farida!' Jess sighs,
throwing her hand across her forehead.
'Who knows the secrets of your wandering mind,
who knows what tales you have to share!'

I punch her in the arm.
'Seriously, Jess,'
I say, and then ...

WHACK!

A loud sound hits the ground
making us both jump back
as a wet wad of toilet paper lands at our feet,
and Jess shouts:
'That nearly hit us!'

I look up,
and my insides sink with dread,
as I see Harry poised on his bike,
eyes staring us down,
daring us to say something.

Jess looks at me, alarmed,
and I look down,
not saying anything.

Harry spins forward,
front wheel in the air,
as if that's what he wanted —
both of us smaller, and quiet —
while he laughs, cycling away.

As we walk back to class,
we both pretend Harry's Special Hello
didn't rattle us.

I take a deep breath,
and try and say the thing that's been on my mind
ever since yesterday:
'Grandma's never time-travelled
my dad before. Like,
it came out of nowhere.
It's just her memory, right?'

Hope tingles at the edge of my question,
but Jess's reply is written all over
her face.

It's the one look I've never been able
to take:
pity.

When someone looks at you,
and their eyes
their smile
the way they phrase
each sentence carefully,
their voice softer,
no matter what words they say,
all add up to what they really mean:
'I feel sorry for you.'

And I don't want them to.

So, when I see those words forming
in Jess, I drop the subject.

HISTORY

We take the stairs to history class
two at a time.

When I first came to high school
I thought it would be fun:
the school like a maze,
filled with secrets to discover.

But all I've found so far
are empty crisp packets on the floor,
and, once, the whole corridor full of water
because someone had blocked
the toilets with paper
and then flushed them.

Jess called it 'The Great Flood'.
At that same time in history
we were learning about 'The Great War',
and I kept thinking that neither of those things
seemed great. How *Great* wasn't the word I'd choose.

Words are important to me.
You've got to get them right.
Words can pin down who someone thinks they are,
or were. They can steer your fate,
or open up your life.

'WELCOME, CLASS. SETTLE DOWN,'

says Mr Harkin.
I like the way he says 'down',
his accent from a place called Belfast.
I asked Mum to show me it on a map,
and she did.

It's like he drops his 'O',
the letter moving down the line
like the word it is trying to show:
welcome class,
settle d   wn.
     oooooo
And we do.

'When we look at the past,' Mr Harkin says,
'it helps us understand where we are now,
and where we're going next.'

He draws a line on the board,
and I picture it expanding into years.

'The history of a place can help us understand its today,
because everything adds up —
all history is a series of yesterdays.
All of them leading us here to today.'

Mr Harkin's classes always start like this:
with a speech to help us see
how important history is.

Last week, he did a lesson on apartheid
in South Africa, and Jess whispered:
'Wait, isn't that near where your family are from?'

I whispered back: 'Zimbabwe.'

Mr Harkin put pictures from South Africa up on the board,
talking about how the white government
oppressed people who were Black and Brown.

Jess nudged my arm:
'Did that happen to your family, too?'

I didn't know what to say.
Grandma used to talk about it —
'Those were hard, hard times,'
she'd said, talking about how the authorities
separated people into categories,
sometimes splitting up whole families,
saying where you could go,
who you could love.

I looked down at my hands,
half Mum, half Dad,
wondering which one of them
the government would have put me with
or if they would have split
me   in   two.

That was when I remembered
something else Grandma used to say,
about being mixed:
'Our family —
we're Southern African and Indian and Arab and Malay.
We're from everywhere,' she'd say.
And then she'd hug me close.
'And that is just one of the many ways
to be from Zimbabwe.'

I wrapped her words around me,
warm as a hug.
But after the lesson,
Jess's questions went on and on:
Was it like that too in Zimbabwe?

What happened to your family?
Were they put in categories? Which one?
Until I felt like I was the one
on the history board,
someone else trying to determine
who I am in *their* eyes,
not mine.

I wanted to explain that Grandma
isn't a statistic on a form,
but the person who gives the best cuddles.
That her stories aren't for other people
but for me — to know where I'm from
by knowing my family.
That when she tells me about Zimbabwe
she tells me about trees with purple blossoms,
and night skies so dark you can see every star —
and it feels like it's not the Zimbabwe of a map or a book
but the Zimbabwe of Grandma's heart.

As I settle into class today,
I think about how if I was gonna do a speech
like Mr Harkin, then maybe I'd try to say
what it's like having this whole history a part of you,
but no one to explain it.
Having others make assumptions about you,
and not knowing how to correct them.
Others asking you questions,
seeing history as something that is yours,
but not knowing how to talk about it,
not knowing how to claim it.

TERM HISTORY PROJECT

Mr Harkin draws my attention back to class
by tapping on the board, in what I think
is meant to be a drum roll.

'Time for our term project!'
he says, and Mr Davis's reminder flashes in my mind:
Maybe Mr Harkin's history project
can help improve your grades.

'Now,' Mr Harkin says,
'has anyone ever heard of a family tree?
Perhaps you've done one yourselves?'

He loads up a presentation on the board,
showing us an image with a map of faces
around the words: 'Harkin Family Tree'.

'Mr Harkin,' someone shouts,
'your great-granddad looks just like you!'

'Very funny,' Mr Harkin says,
then looks at the board again.
'Though, actually, I can kinda see it.
Maybe I'll pick him for my version of the project
I'm going to ask you to do.'

As he talks, he starts walking through the class,
and I get out my notebook, ready to take notes.

'I want you to focus on your VIPs,' Mr Harkin says.
'Your main players, top dogs, the number-one person
that you want to tell a story about in your family.
Take your presentation from there:
tell us about them,
and how they help make you,
you.'

'Sir?' Jess's hand shoots straight up.
'Do you want us to write about *all*
our favourite people?
Just that I have quite a lot?'

Mr Harkin shakes his head:
'No, just the one.'

'Does it have to be, like,
ancestors type family?'
Jess gestures to Mr Harkin's
great-grandfather twin.
'For example, my dad is *technically*
my step-dad, so he doesn't look like me,
and he'll probably never give me a kidney,
not that I think I'll ever need one,
though if I did I bet it would be like
that storyline I saw in a film once
where this woman met the love of her life
and then—'

'Jess?' Mr Harkin says.

'Yes! Oh, sorry, yeah, basically,
I just wanted to say that family
doesn't have to be, like, "blood", right?
Like, I don't really think it matters
if you share the same DNA or whatever,
when you share the same memories,
and, sir, this MVP thing—'

'VIP — Very Important Person.'

'Yeah, that thing, can it be my dad?
Though my mum's super interesting too,
and don't start me on Great-Auntie Enid.'

Mr Harkin smiles as he speaks. 'Great point, Jess.
The person you choose should be someone
important to you, and it's exactly as Jess says ...'
Jess sits up tall at this, and looks around
to make sure everyone notices.
'Family, it's not about DNA,
it's about more than that: love—'

someone at the back groans,

'—and connection and, yes, Jess,
it can even be memory.
It's about the people who inspire you,
who shape you.'

Mr Harkin returns to his desk and smiles wide at the class.
'I can't wait to see what you produce.'

A QUESTION FROM AN UNRAISED HAND

I know it's meant to be comforting.
But if family is about memory,
where does that leave me?

The A on my grades
I wanted to get for my mum,
and Mr Davis,
and me,
suddenly feels very far away.

I look over at Jess,
bouncing up and down,
excited to do her presentation
about her dad,
and I want to slide my head
into my hands.

THE BELL RINGS

As we walk out of class,
Jess grabs my arm.
'Nyla, this is brilliant!'

I look at her with my facial expression
that Mum calls 'The Killer Stare'.

'Don't you see?' she goes on.
'The history project?
Grandma Farida thinking she saw your dad?
Your mum never wanting to talk about it?
You've got the perfect excuse to ask —
you literally have to research your family for school!
Are you gonna do it, Nyla?
Are you gonna do your presentation on your dad?'

That heavy feeling
that had been burrowing down
— like Mr Harkin's 'O's —
changes.
Twists slightly.
Until it feels more like *Maybe?*
Until it feels more like an opportunity.

LUNCH BREAK

'So,' Jess says, taking the last bite
of what she calls her 'PB and J for Jess' sandwich
(peanut butter and jam, I discovered,
when she offered me a bite),
'I'm sure you've seen the signs around school.
I'm absolutely positive you know what I'm about to tell you.'

'Errrr ...' is all I manage to say.

'It's so exciting, isn't it!
I mean, I know they'd never *usually* let someone in our year
be the lead, and admittedly I've read the script
and I could think of a few tweaks,
and the role is *traditionally* played by a guy
but, please, I'm the best talent this school have ever seen,
and I don't think we should be held back by such sexist things,
and I think this will be my time to shine,
don't you?'

I nod, while mentally scrambling,
trying to remember what I may have seen
on the walls of each hallway or noticeboard.

I wonder if this must be what Grandma feels like,
as I look to the side, and then it hits me:
plastered on each window of the canteen.

'You're talking about the play!'
I exclaim, and Jess looks at me.

'Well, obviously, get with the times
before the times get you!
Are you gonna come and watch me audition?
I'm going for the main part:
Prince Hamlet.'

'Prince?'

'Yes. Or Princess. Whatever.
I feel it. I'm ready to be a star!'

Our school closes at lunch time on Friday.
'I can't stay for long, you know I have to be home for—'

'I know! No grandmas will be harmed in the making of this show.'

For a moment, Jess's voice changes,
and it feels like she's opening a window to herself,
and tentatively inviting me in:
'I know that I'll be great, of course,
but there'll be so many older kids there,
and I don't want to feel silly auditioning
in front of the rest of the school.
Please come? I don't want to be alone.'

I think about how
when you invite someone in,
it's not just a gift,
it's bigger than that: it's trust, too.

'You'll be brilliant,' I say,
looping my arm through hers.
'I can't wait.'

6

POPPING CANDY SPARKS

THE VISITOR RETURNS AGAIN

When I walk into the library,
I see a familiar shape curled up on the bean bags.

'Hey, Ray.' I drop my backpack down.

Ray looks up from his book,
as if he's been jolted from a far-away world.
'Hey!'

'Your arm still not healed then?'
I ask.

He gives it a shake as if testing it out.
'Nah, I think it's another day of reading for me.
Do you come here every day?'

I sit down on the orange bean bag
next to him, giving it a shuffle with my bum:
'Books and bean bags, what's not to love?'
Ray shuffles back in his bean bag,
both of us grinning.
'What about you? What do you usually do?'

'I'm usually at the swimming pool,' he says.

'Really?' The last time I went near a pool
was school swimming lessons in year six.
'Are you on a swimming team or something?
Will they miss you?'

'Nah, I just like it — swimming.'
Ray leans forward, his trousers hitching up,
showing his socks that have astronauts on.
'I like to see how fast I can go,
or how many lengths I can do.
Before I hurt my arm, I was on forty-six —
and you only have to go to sixty
to be close to a mile.'

'That's amazing.'

'I enjoy it. When I'm swimming,
it's just me and the water.'
Ray's face goes all concentrated,
his eyebrows drawing slightly together.
'I take off my glasses, and all I can see is blue.
When I'm swimming like that,
it's like what my uncle said on those stairs:
I feel like I'm flying.'

He looks suddenly shy.
It makes me want to not hide.

'I wish I knew how that felt,' I say.
'Not having anything on your mind.
Though, of course,
learning how to fly would be cool too.'

'Just make sure you have cushioning if you practise,'
he adds, and we share a smile,
before he asks gently:
'What's the stuff in your mind?'

I don't know where to start.
There's something in me
that feels like a tangled ball of wool —
Mr Harkin's project on family history,
Jess's questions about Zimbabwe,
the way Harry twists my name.

'There aren't really that many other
kids like me, mixed kids, at my school,'
I begin. 'I just. Do you know how —
do you ever feel ...'

'Alone?' Ray offers. 'Judged?
Like there's stuff that happens
that's not okay but that no one else gets?
Misunderstood?'

I throw my arms up in the air with a sigh.
'All of the above.'

I TRY TO FIND THE WORDS

'It's like, in history,
my teacher was talking about South Africa,
and then my friend was asking about Zimbabwe,
where my dad's family are from,
and it's like everyone —
okay, not everyone, but kinda everyone —
expects me to know every detail of where I'm from.
But I don't.'

It feels important to get it out,
to speak how I'm feeling even just for me.

'I feel like I'm being asked
to be like a ... a spokesperson
for someone else to listen to.
Like, if I want to find out
about where my family is from,
then I want to do it for me,
not for someone else
because they have questions.
Does that make sense?'

Ray nods, a listening smile in his brown eyes.
With each nod it feels like the thread
unspooling in my chest.

'Completely,' he says.
'I get that a lot, too.
It feels like people have an idea of you,
and everything else,
and they're always putting it on you,
when you just wanna figure out how to be you.'
He shakes his head.
'Man. Some people are *fools*.'

My laugh feels big and unexpected in my mouth.

'You sound just like my grandma,' I say,
fool one of her often-used words.
Ray's grin back is shy but warm.

We pause, and look at each other,
sharing a small smile.

'How come you just ... get all of this?'
I ask.

'I think about it a lot,' Ray says,
shuffling closer as he talks.
'Because of stuff that happens to me,
because of the stories my uncle tells me
about when he first came over from Jamaica,
or about how racism changed his life.
Dad's always telling me about history,
and Mum, she's part of this book group ...'

Ray laughs slightly, leaning forward.
'Okay, so it's *meant* to be called "Sisters Who Read"
but *I* call it "Aunties Who Read",
because it's total auntie vibes,
and Mum always takes me along to their parties
where there's mutton curry
and chicken patties and this one auntie,
she *always* brings roti canai
because she knows it's my favourite.'
Ray sighs happily, his face glowing.
'By the end I'm more food than boy.'

'I've never heard of anything so amazing
in my entire life,'
I say, and it's true.

Ray grins. 'It's like ...'
— he tilts his head to one side, thinking —
'like those wetsuits people wear

to swim in the sea. It covers you
and keeps you warm inside,
and keeps out anything else.
Okay, it sounds kinda weird but
that's how the book-club aunties make me feel —
them, and my uncle's stories.'
Ray grins. 'He likes to say *fool*, too.'

I can feel my smile in the corners of my cheeks,
half of me wishing I had something like that,
the rest eager for Ray to tell me more.
'What's your favourite one
of your uncle's stories?'

'There are too many!' Ray exclaims.
'Plus, it's not just the story,
but the feeling you get with it.
The way he talks about Jamaica,
I almost feel like I'm there,
and I can't wait to visit one day.'

I can tell from the look in Ray's eyes,
and the shine in his smile,
that he's feeling some of that special feeling now
just talking about it.

Ray grins. 'I definitely know
what he would say in *this* situation though,
or whenever I struggle with things other people say.'

Ray clears his throat,
and says in the same voice he did yesterday —
'*People don't want to see
the truth that's right in front of them,
and they don't want to hear
the stories that make them uncomfortable,
but that doesn't change the fact
that it's there whether they
like it or not.*'

Ray draws out different words as he speaks,
his hands gesturing with emphasis,
until it feels like his uncle is there in the library with us.

'He always says: *"Raymond! In this world,*
there are shovels, and there are stories.
The moment someone tries to bury your *story*
with their *shovel,*
that's when you know they're not helping you with gardening,
but they're trying to silence your story for good!"'

Ray adds a dramatic thump on the bean bag,
making both of us laugh.
I look up and see the librarian
glancing over —
but she's smiling, too.

Ray goes on, his uncle's voice
big and bold in his mouth
and it wraps around me
filling me with warmth:
'*But if you take it out of their hands,*
if you plant your *story for* yourself —
there's always some metaphor with him —
get good people around to water it,
good ground, that's when it blooms,
and becomes bigger than you.'

As Ray speaks,
it's like the room around us goes quiet.
I sit back, picturing Ray's uncle planting seeds
of stories that turn into trees,
making shade for other people
to sit under and rest.

'Your uncle sounds like the best.'

Ray grins. 'He is. Are your family the same?'
He looks at me curiously.
'Do your parents talk to you about this stuff?'

'My grandma used to,' I say,
with a smile. 'But lately ...
not so much. My mum tries,
but she's busy with ...
other stuff.
And my dad' —
I take a breath,
like it can somehow lift up
the words that feel so heavy in me —
'he passed away when I was little.'

Ray nods as he listens.
'He's the one you would have wanted to ask?'

'Yeah. And now, at school, we've got to do a history presentation
on an important person in our family and our lives,
and I was thinking I'd do it on him.
But, I just ...' I look away, running my hands
up and down the zip of my backpack.
'I don't know where to start.
Like the teacher said this whole thing about memories,
and people who shape our lives.
And I feel like he's hardly a memory ...
but he has shaped my life all the same—?'
Even if that shape is a hole,
I think, but don't say it.

'I ... can I ask ... like ... how did he ...?'
Ray asks gently.

Usually,
whenever anybody asks me about my dad,
their questions feel like a too-tight jumper,
itchy on my skin,

and clawing at my neck.
But with Ray,
it feels like breathing something out,
rather than holding everything in.

'He died in a car accident when I was four.'
Doubt tickles at the back of my mind,
as I remember Grandma on Sunday
saying she saw him in the car park.
I shake my head as if shaking it out.
'I don't really remember much from that night,
except, sometimes, I have this vague memory
of it being late at night and I can hear crying,
and someone with big hands is holding me back,
but ...' I sigh, my shoulders heavy in a half-shrug.
'I'm probably imagining it.'

Ray is quiet for a while, as we both think.
When he looks up, his face isn't pity.
'Thank you for telling me.'

I can tell he means it.

HOPE

'It's important to have someone to talk to
about this stuff,' Ray says,
as I pick up my bag and reluctantly get ready to go.
'Like my uncle: he's someone who understands.
When something happens,
he can tell me it's not okay.
He always makes me feel like ...'
Ray pauses as if thinking,
before saying with a triumphant smile:
'Like the world is a better place because he's in it.
That's why I'm always wanting to do things to help him,
because maybe I'd like to be like him, one day —
and make his world, or someone's world, better too.'

I look down at Ray's arm,
resting in its cast.
'Even if it *occasionally* backfires?'

Ray laughs. 'Yeah.
Definitely taking
"moving heavy objects up flights of stairs"
off my "happy to help" list.
But I guess what I'm saying is,
if you ever want to chat,
you know where I am.'

It's like an open hand
reaching out.
My reply is soft,
as it takes his:

'Thank you. I know —
I know you've got loads of people,
like a whole book club full,
that you can chat to,
but' — my smile feels shy,
but true: 'You can talk to me, too.'

Ray grins. 'I'd love that.
Finally, a friend my own actual age,'
he says, and then we are both laughing
so loud that I swear, behind the desk,
I hear a little laugh from the librarian,
too.

THE CLOCK STRIKES 4

'Grandma says hi,' I say to the librarian,
when I load my books on the desk,
and she beams.

'Tell her I say hi back.' She reaches out her hand,
the beads on her purple cardigan
sparkling as she moves.
'Esmerelda Haldi, at your window-waving service.'

The way her name feels in my mind,
and my chat with Ray,
is like that time Jess and I ate popping candy,
and it filled our whole mouths:
fizzles and sparks.

'Your name is Miss *Haldi*?'
It's familiar from recipes Grandma used to cook,
and letters scribbled on to spice jars.
'Like *turmeric*?'

'Yes.' She laughs. 'Exactly that.'

'But *my* name is Elachi,' I say,
and she leans forward with a wink.

'I know, I've seen your library card.'

'I've never met anyone with a name like me before,'
I say.

'Me too.'

The library feels fuller in my heart today
than it ever has: Ray and Miss Haldi
shining together, popping candy sparks.

BARRICADE

I push the library door, and notice through the glass
a familiar shape,
walking out of the newsagent's opposite.

He looks up at the same time I do.
What's he doing here?

The same shorn blond hair
the same brutish brittle Harry,
and he smiles at me,
and it is not *hello*
but *threat*.

Behind me, a hand pats my shoulder,
makes me jump,
and I spin around to see Ray,
peering out alongside me.

'Wow,' Ray says.
'That boy really knows how to stare.'

'Yeah.'

An awkward pause,
as if Ray is teetering on the edge
between asking who Harry is
and knowing that I don't want to say
that outside is a bully,
and that I'm afraid.

'I had an idea about your family history project,'
Ray says, as Harry makes a slow swagger
towards the library steps,
and I try to figure out how to get out quick.
'Perhaps I can walk you home,
tell you what I was thinking?'

I look up at Ray,
and I think Harry sees it too, on my face,
as I say yes: it is the look of *hope*.
It is the look of *friend*.

When we walk out of the library,
Harry has loped off,
scowling.

RAY'S SUGGESTION

On the walk home,
I learn more about Ray —
from the story behind his astronaut socks
(a gift from his dad)
to his favourite popcorn
(sweet and salted).

When we get to my street,
Ray says, 'Oh,
that's what I wanted to tell you ...'
and my mind is drawn back to the library,
wondering what it means that Harry now knows
I hang out there.

'Last year,' Ray is saying,
'my mum decided to
look for our family history.
She came across her great-grandma's
birth certificate from, like,
a billion years ago.'

'That's so cool, Ray!'

'It totally was.
I was thinking —
maybe if you found your dad's birth certificate,
you could use it as part of your presentation?'

My smile grows wide.
'That is an excellent suggestion, Ray.'

PROMISES FROZEN IN TIME

AFTERNOON INVESTIGATIONS

At home,
I read Grandma poetry
from one of my library books.
It's something we used to do together,
before her time-travelling began.

'Read it again, Sweetie.' She smiles at me.
I do, making my voice more and more grand
until we are both giggling.

When I turn the page,
read her another,
she leans her head back,
and closes her eyes,
resting her hand gently on mine.
'I remember this one,' she says,
finishing the last line with me,
our voices merging.

It's like having her fully back.
Like she's left Alzheimer's
in another time.

After we finish,
I think about Ray's suggestion.
I could make my presentation a mix of
stories and facts about my dad.

'Grandma,' I whisper,
'do you want to help me do some investigating?'

'Oh, if you like, Sweetie,' she chuckles.
I don't know if she fully gets it
but when I drag the Very Important Documents Folder
out from Mum's room,
I set it down in front of us both.

'What have you got down there?'
Grandma asks, as I lay the documents
out on the floor:
Mum's birth certificate in one corner,
mine in the other,
and Mum's parents' death certificates in a third
(they died before I was born).

'It's a bit of our history, Grandma,
my birth certificate, and hey, maybe even yours, too!'

'You were such a tiny baby.'
Grandma runs a hand down my hair.
'When I held you close,
you smelt so brand new!'
She sniffs the air,
and sighs, as if she is back there again.

Her smile is huge,
and mine grows even wider with it.

When I find Dad's birth certificate,
I nearly shout. *This is it!*

'Grandma, look,' I say, 'it's Dad's one, too!'
and then worry, maybe, that I've upset her
mentioning my dad.

But instead, she grins.
'He looked just like you, Sweetie.'

Her words warm me
as I scramble over to my school bag,
and copy the certificate
in my notebook
word for word.

KEEP DIGGING

'What was Dad like as a kid, Grandma?'
I ask, as I leaf through the folder.

'Oh, he was cheeky,' Grandma says,
then leans forward, kissing my head.
'But we loved him very much.'

There's so much I want to ask.
I reach the end of the documents folder —
then realise there's no other certificates in there.

'That's weird,' I say,
and double check again,
looking at my mum's parents' death certificates,
and looking at mine, Mum's and Dad's birth certificates.
'There's no death certificate for Dad.'

'PAH!'

Grandma shouts with a scoff,
and I jump, before kicking myself
for not being more sensitive.
'Oh, don't worry, Grandma, I was just looking ...'

'You were looking for Basim,' she says,
and I pause, her brown eyes direct in mine.
She seems so completely herself still,
but something within me feels like we're teetering
on the edge of unknown territory.

I answer simply with the truth:
'Yes. I was looking for ...'
it comes out as a whisper,
'his death certificate.'

'Well, you won't find it,'
she says with a huff, and another. 'Pah!
I can tell you one thing for sure:
he's not dead.'

The room freezes, fractures,
opens up again.
I swear for a second
the clock by the window
pauses in its tick,
holding us together,
before moving forward again as I try to speak:

'Grandma, what do you mean?'

Every beat of my heart
is latched to her face
to the clearness of her eyes
trying to figure out if she is speaking
from now
or from another time.

'We need to find him,' she says,
her voice dropped to a whisper now,
as if she's scared someone may overhear.

'Find my dad? Grandma, he — he passed away—?'

She leans down from her chair,
grasping my hands in hers.
'No! He's out there, somewhere.
We mustn't tell anyone. Basim ran away
that night. Oh, there was a terrible argument,
and he ran away, and we need to bring him home.'

'Is this — Grandma — I know it's hard but please try:
do you mean that night when I was small?
Is this what you meant
when you said you saw him the other day?'

'He ran away!' Grandma insists.
'Listen to me, we need to find him.
Can you do that?'

Her eyes are so sincere,
their brown circling within mine,
as we look at each other.

'Can you find him for me?
Can you bring him home?'

THE TRUTH

I don't know what to do.
So, I say:
'Yes, Grandma.
I'll find him.'

She smiles.
Leans back in her chair.
Replies:
'Our secret.'
And then:
'Thank you.'

WHEN I GO TO BED THAT NIGHT

All I can think is:
There was no death certificate
for my dad anywhere to be found.
Why?

All I can hear is
Grandma's voice:
'We mustn't tell anyone.
Will you find him for me?'

All I can feel is
the trait I have inherited from my mum:
We never break a promise —
and the awful feeling that I have to keep something from her,
in order to keep true to her, to us.

'Yes, I'll find him.'

My own words whisper back to me like a ghost.

8

WORDS LIKE TICKING CLOCKS

GRANDMA'S WORDS

Grandma's words keep me company all day:
they are all I see on the board in maths,
they are between the lines of my notebook,
and the bounce of the balls in P.E.
Dead?
      Not Dead.
            Dead?
                  Not Dead.

At break, when Jess is chatting
about her upcoming audition
her voice feels so far away
that I hardly hear it
over the drumbeat of Grandma's still in my mind.

When I get to the library,
Ray looks up
but then his face freezes,
when he sees mine.
I can see it too
when I get close,
reflected in his lenses:
my face long,
like how Mum's looked the other night,
my eyes big and tired.

Something about seeing myself
and the fact that Ray doesn't know my family
makes the words come rushing out:

'I did what you suggested,
I looked through my mum's important documents folder
and I found my dad's birth certificate
but I couldn't find the one from, you know,
the death certificate —
the one that you get when someone's died.'

'No waaaay,' Ray says,
leaning in, and I realise
that we are whispering,
under Miss Haldi's watchful eye.

She waves, and we both smile,
like everything's okay,
and there's nothing we're trying to hide.

'Do you think she just lost it?'
Ray asks, 'Or—'

'Definitely *Or*. I asked my grandma,
and then *she* started saying
that he's not dead—'

'Wait, what?'

'—and that he ran away and that it's a secret.
Please don't tell anyone, Ray ...'

'I won't—'

'And that she needs me to find him—?'

Ray's eyes are as round as his glasses,
two orbs spinning,
taking it all in.
'I mean, if this is true,
why hasn't your grandma told you before now?
What're you gonna do?'

How to explain: that with Alzheimer's
it's like it lets Grandma's guard down,
so that as well as travelling through time,
sometimes it means that she feels freer to tell
everybody what she thinks —
like back at the supermarket,
when she ploughed that woman down,
and didn't give what Jess would call
a 'shiz'.

'It's complicated,' is all I manage to say,
feeling too exhausted to explain Grandma's fading,
fantastic memory.

'Hmm.' Ray looks at me.
I'm scared that he'll laugh.
'Okay,' he says instead,
with a little smile.
'Where do we begin?'

I reach into my bag with relief,
just as the sound of a sudden smash,
like the tinkling of breaking glass,
followed by
a loud shrill noise
fills the room.

Ray and I both duck instinctively.
Miss Haldi rushes out from behind the desk,
'Don't worry,
don't worry—'

she calls,
as concerned mutters rise from the old ladies
in the corner.
'We must have somehow tripped
the fire alarm—'

Miss Haldi stops mid-sentence,
confused concern on her face as she
looks towards the door
swinging shut,
and the shattered glass on the floor
next to the fire alarm.
'Did anybody see—?'
she says, and then shakes her head,
as she begins ushering us out.

'Will the books be okay?' Ray asks,
his eyes solemn as they look to Miss Haldi.

'Oh, these tomes have been through worse than this!'
Miss Haldi says, though her smile and her eyes
are facing in different directions, like a compass
searching for its way.

'Besides,' she adds,
and when she looks at us her eyes are clear,
like they've found their centre.
'They'll guard the place
while we're outside waiting for the fire brigade.
I'm sure it's a false alarm.'

We rush out together,
Miss Haldi's hands on our backs
gentle and guiding.

OUTSIDE THE LIBRARY

Ray and I stare up at the library building.

'It doesn't look like it's on fire,' he says,
tilting his head to one side.

'Did you see the thing by the door,
the red break-in-case-of-emergency thing?'
I ask. Ray shakes his head.
'It was kinda ... broken?'

'Maybe someone knocked into it coming in?'

I want to agree, but something nudges at me —
something doesn't feel quite right.

Ray watches the fire crew,
who have started to arrive.
'I can't *wait* to tell my uncle about this.'

His words are like a clock,
ticking towards a reminder in my mind:
Family. Grandma. Got to get home.

'I've got to go — but I haven't even shown you
everything I found yet,' I groan.

'Same time tomorrow?' Ray asks,
and then brightens. 'Or even earlier —
my school finishes early on a Friday,
does yours? I usually go to my uncle's,
but he won't mind.'

I hear the small cough
of a familiar throat being cleared:
'I'm so sorry, you two,
but I don't think the library

will be open tomorrow —
we can't open again until we replace the alarm,
and who knows how long that'll take ...'
Miss Haldi breathes out a sigh of frustration.
'At least it was a false alarm,
and we didn't need to get the fire hose!'

She strides back towards the library,
long hair flowing around her.

'Well, there goes that plan,' I say,
turning back to Ray with a shrug.
I can't invite him to my house —
what if he ends up meeting Grandma,
and it's not a good day?

But Ray's eyes are lit up with excitement.
'I know the perfect place!
In the pool building,
they have this whole upstairs bit,
with benches looking down,
it's where my mum and dad sit when I'm swimming.'

The pang I usually feel
when I hear the words 'Mum and Dad'
feels less when I hear Ray say it,
because of the look on his face
when he talks about swimming.
I think that look's name is 'happy'.

'I've been going every now and then,
since I hurt my arm —
it's the closest I can get to being back in the water.'
Ray describes the pool —
it's near the big supermarket
Grandma, Mum and I visit on our Sundays.
'Why don't we meet there?'

'Okay,' I say, after quickly doing
the time maths in my head. 'I'm in.'

Ray grins. 'Great!'

I look up at the library,
filled with fire fighters
dressed in yellow and red,
and Miss Haldi moving through it all —
checking in on the books.

The library's in good hands,
and so am I.

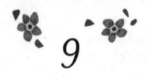

9

GRANDMA BEANS

THAT NIGHT

When I ask Mum if I can go to the pool
with my new friend Ray,
she practically leaps out of her chair.

First come a thousand questions:
who my new friend is,
and how we met, and then
Mum's signature preparations:

'These are the times for the X5 bus, from our usual stop.'
She shows me the way on an app on her phone,
and then scribbles it on a Post-it note,
the same ones she sometimes sneaks
into my bag before school.
'Don't worry, I'll be home for Grandma's drop-off.
How *exciting*, Nyla!'

I haven't seen her look this happy in a long time.

'Mum, chill.' I laugh. 'It's no big deal.'

'It is!' she insists.
'Going on an adventure with a new friend,
it's what your—' and then her voice goes soft,
and I see those familiar lines on her face again,
the ones that weigh so much.

This is it, I think. My chance to ask more.
To tell her about what I'm searching for.

'Mum, about Dad—'

Mum drops a tin of beans on the counter,
the onion next to it rolling off,
and landing on the floor with a thud.
'Oh, gosh, what a mess I'm making,'
she says as she bends to pick them up.

In the living room behind us,
Grandma releases a snort of a snore,
like a reminder:
I promised I wouldn't tell anyone.

And I want to see Mum's face light up again.
Not look heavy, or sad.

So, when she stands up,
I ask a different question:

'Mum, what are we making for tea?'

Mum replies with a grin:
'Grandma Beans.'

GRANDMA BEANS

It's one of the first recipes Grandma taught Mum,
and me.

'Start simple,' she used to say.
'Start with family — with home.
This is a recipe I used to cook for your dad
when he was young
and we didn't have much —
but we had love.'

She smiled her cheeky Grandma smile,
'Just like you, Mum and me.'

The ingredients to her recipe are easy
('And cheap!' Mum would always add):
a tin or two of kidney beans
and whatever spice you have.

'You can go a long way with salt and chilli,'
Grandma whispers in my memory.

In the living room, in now-time,
Grandma loudly snores.

When the time comes to add the chilli to the pan,
Mum looks at me meaningfully.
'Ready?' she asks.

I nod.
'Ready.'

Within a few moments
we start to cough,
chilli caught in our throats.
Cough!
Cough!
Cough!

'That's how you know the spices are working!'
Grandma says in my mind.

In now-time, I hear the sound of a throat clearing
and a voice that is past and present and future all at once:
'Is that my beans I smell?'

Grandma appears in the kitchen doorway,
twinkling her cheeky Grandma smile.

When we serve it
Mum's eyes are tired but happy and round.

Grandma takes a spoonful:
'Mmmmmm!
It's just as good as if I made it myself!'

Mum winks across the table.

I lean my head against Grandma's arm,
her skin cool.

'You did, Grandma,' I whisper.
'You made it in my memory.'

I meet Mum's eye again.
When she clears her throat,
her eyes watering,
I know it's from something
more than chillies.

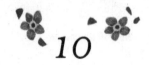

A FEELING BIG AS THE SKY

A CLEAR BLUE SKY

When Ray and I sit down
on the benches above the swimming pool,
the first thing I notice is the sky:
the roof above the pool is made of glass,
with white beams either side.
And when you look up,
all you see is bright blue
smattered with clouds like candyfloss.

'I like looking up, too,'
Ray says, noticing me looking.
'In fact, I think that's how I got so good
at backstroke.'

I look down
at the pool below us,
then to the roof above,
us on the benches halfway between.
'I feel like we're in another world.
It's like being on a cloud.'

My cheeks flush, I sound silly —
but Ray's face has the same look of wonder
that I feel.

'You know how I said I came to the library,
because I sprained my arm?'

'Yeah?'

'Well, that's true, but my mum ...'
Ray's eyes move out on to the shining pool
as he talks. 'She's always trying
to get me to make more friends.
I think she worries that I
spend all my time alone swimming,
or hanging with my uncle —
but I just like what I like,
and what's wrong with that?'
he says with a laugh.

'So, when you needed a new hobby
which involved making friends,
you naturally chose ...'

'... the library?'
Ray finishes,
and we both laugh.

A small grin plays across my face
as I say:
'I mean, it worked!
Though I guess you'll never know if your mum
told me to come to the library.'

An expression of genuine confusion crosses Ray's face —
'That *is* something she would do' —
and then he starts to laugh again,
our voices joining the medley of sound echoing around the pool:
parents cooing and babies splashing and old ladies chatting,
all of it a mish-mash of peaceful noise.

'Did you feel nervous, coming here for the first time?'
I ask, thinking about how brave it is,
and how cool, that Ray does his own thing.

'A bit,' Ray replies.
'Though I wasn't totally alone —
one of the book club aunties has a nephew
who is a lifeguard here,
and he encouraged me to come.'
Ray smiles at the memory.
'The first time I came here,
when I got in the water —
all the noise of other people's chatter
became so quiet.'
Ray leans back, and I do too,
looking up at the reflection of the water,
rippling on the glass roof.
'By the time I got out,
I felt more myself,
and it didn't matter what anyone else thought,
because I knew who I was.'

I nudge him gently.
'The best swimmer this pool has ever seen?'

'Obviously,' he says.

Our eyes meet as we both grin.

'I'm really glad you have a place
that makes you feel this way,'
I say.

Ray smiles his soft-shy Ray smile.
'I like hanging out with you,' he says,
while in the pool below someone jumps in
with a splash.
'It's like when I'm with my uncle,
or swimming.
You see me as me.'

I look back at him,
the shine of the water dancing across us.
'Any time, Ray,'
I say, and it sounds like a promise,
and one I want to make.

ADVENTURES

The wooden benches bounce underneath
as I turn to Ray, excited:
'Maybe our next adventure
can be going for a swim together,
once your arm is healed?'

Ray bounces the benches back with a jump:
'YES! It's gonna be so much fun!
Or we could even swim in the sea, too.
I've *always* wanted to do that.'

'Let's do it! My grandma always used to say
that a good thing shared is a good thing—'

'—multiplied!' Ray finishes with a laugh.
'My uncle says that too.
Though, hey, we haven't finished the current adventure —
what did you find out about your dad?'

I zip open my backpack,
and pull out my notebook
laying it all out in front of Ray:
my notes about my dad's birth certificate,
and details of what Grandma said.

'This is what I've got so far,'
I explain. 'I don't have much.
A few stories —
though I'm not sure I can find him in them.
I don't know any of his friends,
I know he was a nurse — but not
where he worked.
Though I'm guessing it was where
we used to live,
before we moved away shortly after ...'

I suddenly don't know what words to use.
He died? He disappeared?
Ray's eyes move sympathetically
between me and my notebook,
pushing his glasses further up his nose.

'Maybe we could look for
hospitals where you used to live?'
Ray suggests.

'Yeah. Maybe there'll be someone
there who knows something.'

'Exactly!' Ray pulls out his phone.
'Do you want to do it?
It's your project, after all.'

I look at Ray's phone in his outstretched hand,
and think about how this is a big trust,
and how maybe it's because he knows
how much this means to me —
that I need to be the one pressing the buttons,
and finding the answers first.
'Are you sure? Thanks, Ray.'

We huddle over the phone together,
as I type in:
Hospitals in Hillworth.

'Oh, Hillworth, cool,
that's where—'
Ray says, then stops
as the words *Hillworth District General Hospital*
fill the phone screen.

'I think this is it,' I whisper.
'But we need to be sure.'
I go back to the search page,

the sounds of splashes and shouts
reverberating in the background,
as I type in:
Hillworth District General, Basim.

Beside me, Ray takes in a deep breath.

The first listing is a blog page:

'... pictured left to right, Hillworth District General's
(HDG) nursing team after raising money
for the charity marathon: Mo,
Basim, Amina ...'

My hands freeze,
as Ray and I look at each other,
eyes wide.

Ray reaches forward slowly and taps on the link,
his hand shaking as much as mine,
and then there,
right in the centre of the picture:

'That's him, Ray,'
I whisper.
'That's my dad!'

FOLLOWING THE LEAD

Ray holds the phone close to his face,
then looks at me,
shock written all over it.

'He ...' Ray stumbles,
as he passes the phone back to me.
'He kinda looks like you.'

'I know,' I whisper back.

'This page is from, like, ten years ago,' Ray says.
'Is that before, you know, he passed away?
Like, I don't think this proves anything—?'

But all I can do is stare at the picture,
wanting to print it into my mind:

the way my dad tilts his head back as he laughs,
a marathon T-shirt on his chest,
his hands held high in the air
with two people either side of him:
a man who is looking off camera,
and a woman who is laughing,
her warm eyes looking at him.

'Her,' I say to Ray,
tapping her face on the screen,
and squinting at her name.
'Amina. We need to find her.'

We search again —
Ray's knee jigging nervously next to mine —
this time replacing my dad's name
with Amina's.
Within seconds, we're on a staff page
for the HDG.

Ray's voice comes out in a whisper of disbelief as he reads:
'*Sister Amina Brown: head of nursing.*
She still works there.'

My heart beats so fast it feels
like it could run straight out of me.

'Ray,' I say. 'Do you think it would be possible
for me to make a Dad-related emergency phone call?
Or maybe not, sorry. I can wait until I'm home.'

Ray's face is full of something like awe,
his mouth hanging open for a moment before he utters:
'Of course. Maybe she can tell you ...
what she knows. Nyla—'
He stops, his face searching
as if looking for what to say.
'Good luck.'

My smile is tight as I whisper:
'Thank you.'

I rush towards the stairs,
leaving the sounds of the pool
and its reassuring, rippling bubble
behind.

Outside, hands shaking,
I look at the picture
on the staff page one more time:
it's definitely her, Amina from the photo,
just slightly older,
and her hair is shorter than it was back then.

I scroll down to the hospital phone number.
Press *Call*.

'HELLO, HILLWORTH DISTRICT GENERAL HOSPITAL, HOW MAY I—?'

'Hello!' My breath comes out in shaky puffs.
'I'd like to speak to a nurse, to Nurse Amina Brown, please?'

'Aaaaaannnd may I ask who is calling, please?'
the voice on the other line trills.

'Yes, it's her — relative. That's me.'

There's a beep as the call is transferred,
and then after a wait that feels like forever,
a smooth voice answers:

'Hello, Sister Brown speaking—?'

'Is that Sister *Amina* Brown?'

'Yes, how may I help you?'

'Hi! I — hi! Erm, I wondered if I could
just ask you a quick question
about someone you used to work with—?'

'Who is this? The front desk said something about a relative—?'

'Ah, not quite, well,
you know, we're all relatives in the world, really,
but it's important, if I could just have a minute of your time—'

'Now, girl, you sound too young to be a journalist—'

'It's about Basim!' I say, my dad's name rushing out
with an exhalation of breath. 'Basim Elachi,
you used to work with him. I wondered, maybe,
if you were friends with him,
if you—'

'Basim?' she says.
'Why do you want to know about Basim?
Where did you get that name?'

'Do you know him? Did you — is he —
do you know where I can find him,
or do you have any information about him?'

Her breath comes out in
a short sharp gasp
on the end of the phone,
like the ones Jess makes
when we watch horror movies
and something jumps out unexpectedly.
'I can't ... answer ... any of your questions.'
Her voice is shaky, strained and formal.

'Wait, please — I know you knew him,
know him ... please,
I need to know what happened!'

Her silence is so loud.

'Please, Sister Amina,'
I whisper.

'I'm sorry,'
she says.

And then she hangs up the line.

SILENCE

I try calling back,
telling the receptionist that we got cut off.
But the phone just rings and rings,
until it vanishes
just like Amina's voice.

I walk back into the pool building,
and it looks darker than before,
rain clouds flying above us through the huge window.

Ray's phone hangs heavy in my hand.
I can feel the past tugging at me,
pulling me towards things I don't understand,
or know, but want to.

Ray picks nervously at his sling.
I must have taken super long on the phone:
when I left, both our bags were spread out over the benches,
spilling with our stuff,
but he's packed his back up.

'What did she say?' Ray asks.

I pass him back his phone.
'Nothing. She didn't want to talk to me.
She hung up.'

Ray's face — usually as open as his laugh —
looks serious.

'Thanks for letting me call, Ray.

I just got so caught up,
seeing the picture and — I just —
I feel like Amina's hiding something,
like I'm so close to uncovering something,
I just don't know which direction to go in—'

'I think—' Ray starts, his body jiggling nervously,
'maybe, maybe you're looking in the wrong place,
or maybe — maybe things aren't always as they seem,
or maybe, maybe your grandma—'
He suddenly stands up with a jolt.
'I don't know, maybe, I don't know.'

He looks like he's about to spontaneously combust.

'Are you okay?' I ask,
as Ray picks up his backpack,
carrying it with his free hand.

'I'm sorry,' he says,
with a whoosh of release, as if admitting defeat.
'I've got to go, but you'll get home okay, right?'

I have sudden déjà vu
to the conversation with Sister Amina
on the phone.
Why does nobody want to speak to me?

'Did I do something wrong?'
I reach out to him.
'I'm sorry about borrowing your phone—'

'No, it's fine, I ...' Ray rushes past me,
and then looks back,
his face full of an emotion I can't read.
'I've got to go.'

He vanishes without
another word.

And I'm alone
with the sound of the pool's echoes
and the smell of its chlorine
and a feeling in my chest
bigger than the sky.

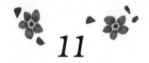

11

GRANDMA IS NOT THE ONLY ONE WHO FORGETS

DEFLATED

I sit down on the benches.
Disappointment,
like a balloon shrinking,
releasing all its air.

Maybe I'll see Ray at the library next week —
but then Miss Haldi said she didn't know
when it would open again.

The sky feeling widens —
more cry than yawn.
I miss my safe place.

I gather my things,
thumping my notebook back in my bag
from where I'd been showing Ray my notes.
Was it because I showed him too much?
All this stuff, stuff I didn't want to tell Mum,
or Jess —
        and then —
                and then —

Shiz,

shiz, shiz, shiz,
I think, Jess's voice coming in my mind.
Shiz.

I forgot.
Jess's audition.
It was today.

I look at the clock:
she'll have already been
and gone.

Something shakes
in the corners of my mouth.

I think of Mum's face, how happy she was
when I told her about Ray —
that I'd made a new friend.

And how I forgot Jess's audition
after she asked me to come.

The shake in my mouth turns into a wobble
in my jaw, as I try not to let the sky-big-feeling
take over me, as it threatens to lift me up,
and carry me away.

RING RING

When I get home,
I try calling Jess's house.
I know her number off by heart.

Jess's mum is hesitant on the phone:
'Sorry, Nyla, love, she's just in a bit of a grump,
but I'll tell her you called.'

'Can you tell her —
can you tell her I'm sorry I missed her audition?
And I bet she was brilliant?
And I can't wait to hear how it went?'

'I will, Nyla. Thanks for calling.'

I hope my message gets through.

ONE THING I CAN'T FORGET

That weekend,
whenever I get Grandma alone,
I whisper questions to her.
I need to find out more about what she knows:
'Grandma,
do you remember what we spoke about?
About finding my dad? Finding Basim?'

Every time, no matter the question,
Grandma looks at me,
and whispers back:
'We can't tell anyone.
We have to find him ourselves.
It's the only way.'

By the time Sunday rolls around,
I feel like I've had a month
not of Sundays,
but of Grandma's face,
urging me to keep my promise.

Solve the mystery, I whisper to myself,
as I lie in bed that night,
trying not to worry about Ray
or Jess not returning my calls.
Find Dad. Help Grandma.
And maybe, I think,
in the process,
understand who I am.

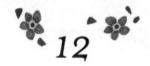

12

IN MY HEAD, I KNOW
WHAT I WANT TO SAY

SORRY

I try in registration
to grab Jess's attention
but every time I whisper her name
or nudge her arm
she turns her face away.

At break, when I go up to her,
and try to explain,
she says, 'Oh, I'm sorry,
I only speak to friends who keep promises.
Excuse me,' and walks away.

I wish I could tell her,
that's exactly what I was doing —
just not to her.

Before science,
I try explain my reasons:
'I'm sorry,' I say,
'I found something important out about
my history project. You were right, Jess.
And I'm so sorry I didn't make it.'
I see an intrigued glint in her eye,
but she turns her head away.

At lunch, I go to our usual table,
and wait for Jess to join,
but she doesn't.
I spend the hour alone,
looking up at the door,
hoping she'll walk through,
with her PB and J for Jess sandwiches,
and all her jokes.

I really *do* want to know,
how her audition went.

I really *would* have loved
to see her
dazzle
on stage.

I WALK HOME ALONE

I walk out of school with my head low.
Up ahead, I see the bob of Jess's backpack,
and feel a pull — I'm about to chase after her,
to try to explain, to try and figure out if I should tell her
what I found out about my dad,

when I feel
                    a shove
                              against my shoulder,
                    and then
Harry is in my face,
his face sneering as he pushes me again:

'Nyyyyyyla, Nyyyyyla, Pants On Fire,
Have you got ants in your pants,
is that why they gave you that name?'

Something about the name he calls me
tugs at a place far back in the tangled muddle
of emotions in my head.

'Go away,' I mumble
in a way that feels brave,
while thinking:
Please don't do anything worse.

'Saw you sitting alone at lunch,
seems like you lost your only friend.
I bet she wanted to hang out with someone
with a normal name for a change.'
He shoves my shoulder again.
'What's wrong, Nyyyyyyyyyyeeeeeeeelllllllaaaaaarrrrr?
Am I saying it right? Nyyeeellllarrrr
NYEEEELLLAARRR
NYYYEEEELAAARRRRRRRRRRRR!'

'Shut up!' I say, at the exact same time
another voice joins its chorus with mine:
'Back off!'

Suddenly an arm links with my own.
And the familiar face of Jess
is warm,
as it replaces Harry's shove.

'Whatever,' he says,
and sticks two fingers up
as he jumps on his bike
and cycles off.

'Ignore him, Nyla,' Jess says softly,
and huddles close to me.

FRIENDS

Jess and I walk home.
And though she said to ignore Harry,
we can't — his words hovering around us,
neither of us sure what to do — holding us down
while at the same time blowing away
the tension of our silence.

'I like your name, Nyla,' Jess says at last,
as I chew the insides of my cheeks.

'Me too,' I whisper.

'I don't get it, like, why does he always pick on you?'

'Because I'm not white like him,
and sometimes I think
because I'm not rich like he is, either.
And because he's trying to hurt me,
and he thinks that's how to do it.'

Jess makes a thoughtful *hmm*.

'I think that's racist,' she says,
as if just figuring something out.

'I think it is, too,' I reply,
and the admission feels like a heavy stone
moving through my body,
and settling inside.

I try to make my voice sound defiant:
'He doesn't get to decide what my name means,
or how you say it.'

'He doesn't,' Jess agrees,
then turns to me with a glint in her eye.
'*Maybe* we should turn it into the name
of your superhero alter-ego.'
Jess lowers her voice dramatically,
sweeping her hand through the air:
'Nyelar — Conqueror of Bullies,
and Mistress of Time.'

At this I have to laugh,
and soon the laugh has moved up my body,
lifting that stone up with it,
as the pair of us giggle and snort,
and I wonder if this feeling
could become something else,
transform into something bigger,
yet more true to itself:
like a cry.
Or a scream.
Or a howl.
Or a laugh.

APOLOGY

'I'm sorry, Jess,' I say,
and she shakes her head.

'I'm sorry, too — I've been more
shiz-biz than showbiz today.'
I try not to start laughing again.
'I know you wouldn't have missed it on purpose.
I meant to make it up to you at lunch,
but then Ms Mills called me to an emergency play meeting,
and by the time I made it out,
you'd gone.'

There's a small, soft release in my chest.
Harry was wrong — about so many things,
and this: I do have a friend.

'It's just, well, I kinda missed you,' Jess says.
'I wanted my pal there.'

'I know. I really did want to cheer you on,
and I really do want to know how it went—?'

'I got the main part!' Jess squeals.
'I found out in the meeting today! Apparently
they loved my idea of me as Hamlet,
because it's *genius*, obviously.
Rehearsals start next week.'

Jess strikes a pose as we reach my front door,
hand on hips, face grinning, eyes wide.
'What do you think?
Am I the future of British film and TV?
A young star from the North,
ready to take on the world?'

The truth feels easy as I say:
'Definitely.'

Jess grins,
and hugs me.
'You're a star too,'
she says.

QUESTIONS I'D ASK MY DAD

When I get home I feel lighter.
Like I have a friend.
Sad that people are racist.
Confused about what racism is.
Wanting to curl up inside my library book.
Wishing life was as simple as its chapters and straight lines.

There are so many questions I wish I could ask my dad.
It's not just that I want to solve his mystery,
but that I want him to help me,
with all the things I feel like only he can answer, like:

What did you say when people said racist things to you?
What was growing up like for you?
Did you ask for help when you weren't sure what to do?
Did you have friends to walk you home from school?
Does the questioning get any easier?
Are the answers always hard?
Did you die or did you run away?
Are you a secret?
Will you let me find you?

IN MY HEAD, I WANT HIM TO SAY

'Nyla: you are enough.'

It's these words I hold close to me,
that guide me through the rest of the week.
You are enough.

GRANDMA'S BOX OF BUTTONS

STRAY BUTTONS

My Saturday activity with Grandma
is sorting through buttons in her button box.
Maria said it was something we should do
to help keep Grandma's mind active.

Grandma used to tell me stories about her buttons,
and bits of ribbons and lace she keeps in an old biscuit tin.
'Oh, this one I kept from one of your baby dresses!'
she'd say. Or,
'This lace was on my favourite blouse when I was young!'

Today, she holds up a small, hexagonal red button
that is multifaceted and shiny like a jewel.

'There's something I'm forgetting, Sweetie,'
she says, and her face trembles and tremors.

I lay my head on her arm,
closing my hand around the small button,
and hers in it.

'It's going to be okay, Grandma,'
I say.

A promise isn't just a one-time deal:
it's something you have to actively keep up
each and every day.

I HAVE TO ASK

It's something that has been bothering me
all week.
It danced at the edges of my mind,
as Jess and I went from class to class.

It pulled at the corners of my mouth
every time I walked past the closed library,
and looked-not-looked to see if Ray was coming back.

I need to talk to Mum.
To ask her about Dad,
about Sister Amina, Hillworth.

Even if I don't ask her outright,
and betray Grandma's secret,
the whole point of doing my history project on my dad
was so I could ask Mum about him
and find out more.

As I go back upstairs,
one hand on the white painted banister,
the other on Grandma's button box,
taking it back to her room,
I see Mum's bedroom door ajar,
and her sitting on the bed alone.

MUM'S SECRET PHONE CALL

I reach forward to enter the room
when I hear a word
that stills me
as if someone has pressed 'Pause':

'*Basim*.'

Mum's talking about my dad.
She's on the phone,
her back turned away from me.

I creep as close as I can,
trying to hear what she is saying.

'If I do,' she is saying,
'it means telling Nyla about what
Basim did. It would change her life.'

The button box trembles in my hand.
It feels like my life is already changing,
right this minute.

'I make so many promises to other people
but I made one promise to myself:
that Nyla wouldn't have to know this.
I don't want her to worry.'

Mum pauses, listening to the other person
on the phone.

I'm clutching the button box so tightly
that my hands are cramping.

Mum makes an exasperated sound.
'That's not the point.
The point is Basim left—'

And with that, two things happen at once:

The first is the feeling of my heart
— the same one that has been pounding
and hounding me to find the truth —
splitting, as if this moment has hammered it
into tiny shards.

Basim left.

The second is the sound of the muffled cry
of another voice, coming from downstairs.

I look up — Mum hasn't heard —
but the distant cry comes again —

and then I am running away from one person
and one truth,
towards another:

Grandma.

AT THE BOTTOM OF OUR STAIRS

The front door is wide open.
Please no —
I run through it,
and Grandma is standing there
on the front step.

'Basim! Basim!'
she is saying,
clutching at the edges of her cardigan,
and, for a moment,
I wonder if she somehow heard
Mum's phone call,
too.

Grandma looks at me,
her face desperate:
'He was here, Sweetie.
He came back!'

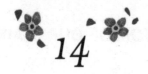

EVERYWHERE, NOWHERE

EVERYWHERE, NOWHERE

Blood rushes in my ears:
beat-beat-beat-BASIM.
I scan the street,
wanting to shout: 'Dad!'
but there's no one there.

'I saw him!' Grandma repeats.
She waves a finger back towards the house.
'I saw him through the window,
and he didn't see me but I ran
to catch him —
but when I opened the door,
poof, he was gone!'

Grandma's voice becomes a low cry,
as she repeats my dad's name again,
the 'eeeeeeeeeeeem' of it
buried in my shoulder
as she lays her head
against me.

I run my hand across her curly plait.
It runs down the front of my jumper
as if it is my own.

I feel like both grandmother
and granddaughter,
one half of me looking after her,
the other half wanting someone
to look after me,
as we both stand in front of the house,
thinking:

Dad?

ALL THIS COMMOTION

Behind us,
I hear footsteps coming down the stairs.

'What's all this commotion?' Mum says,
looking concerned, her gaze moving
between Grandma and me,
as I blurt out a quick:
'Nothing!'

But really, I want to scream.
I want to demand
to know what she is hiding from me,
why she's kept a secret from me,
something that she said
could change my life.

My dad. He left. He's — alive.
And she lied about it.
She's kept it from me for all this time.

But looking at her face,
how much she cares for me and Grandma,
I remember
the other bit she said:
'I made a promise to myself:
I don't want Nyla to worry.'

Mum's one promise that she made to herself,
was about me.
Was *for* me—?
And if she knew that I knew,
and how worried I was —

I don't know what to do,
as it all tangles in me:

the anger

and the love.

AVALANCHE

Mum sighs, and gently takes Grandma's elbow.
'Come on now, Farida.'

My eyes stay down as we turn to go back inside,
the button box still clenched in my hand,
my fingers gripping it tightly
as if it's the only way to hold everything in.

And that's when I see it.

On the edge of the doormat,
pressed up flat against the door:
a small cream envelope,
neatly folded,
resting on the concrete step.
No address.
No stamp.
Only a single letter:

R.

R like Ruth — like my mum's name.

And R like release.

I feel all the fizzing,
sizzling, ready-to-run
emotion in my hands,
the same ones that have me clenching so tight
to the box of Grandma's buttons,
and I release it —
the button box flying out of my grasp,
the lid jumping up to the sky,
as an explosion of colour bursts out,
buttons cascading across the doorstep
an avalanche of loose memories and scraps
held in tiny circles of gold and pink and blue.

'Oh, Nyla!' Mum exclaims,
as Grandma squeaks:
'Oh, Sweetie!'

I jump down, as if to start picking them back up,
covering the envelope with my jumper's sleeve.
'Don't worry, I'll clean up!'

The minute they're both inside,
I shove the letter in my pocket,
where it beats like a pulse.

15

THE LETTER

ALL WEEKEND LONG

It takes all weekend
before I'm alone
and ready to open the letter.
I decided,
if my life was about to change,
that I would wait one more day.
I would have one
last
month of Sundays.

SNAPSHOT OF SUNDAY

When we got home from the big supermarket,
unpacking in the kitchen,
Mum said: 'I've got a surprise.'

Yeah, I thought. *Too right.*

She laid on the kitchen table
a small fondant frog,
its bright green face
and goofy smile glowing
on our sunflower table cloth.

I suddenly felt like crying.

'Sweetie for Sweetie!' Grandma shouted,
then leaned forward, grinning.
'Perhaps you may even share.'

Mum hovered.
'It must be a good day today,'
she whispered, 'either that,
or she has a priority
of what's most important to remember.
If so, you and cake would definitely
be at the top of the list.'

And Dad, I wanted to say.
*And the fact that you're keeping him
a secret from me.*

When I didn't reply,
Mum added gently:
'I wanted to cheer you up.'

But it was already too late,
was already too much
for our month of Sundays.

So, I came up here,
and closed my bedroom door,
pushing my stack of library books against it.

I opened my notebook.
Curved my finger along
the seal of the cream envelope,
the one marked R,
the initial for Mum: Ruth.
The one hand-delivered
at the same time Grandma
went running outside
swearing she saw my dad.

It would change Nyla's life.

Mum's words in my memory
hover above the open envelope,
as if asking me:
Do you really want to read this?
Are you ready for what it says?

I take a deep breath.
Slide out the paper.
And read.

DEAR R,

Sometimes, I walk out by the trees and imagine I can hear the sound of the crickets and it reminds me of you. You come to me always like this: in the small sounds of my imagination, and it makes me feel like you're still here. Like we could still be the family we once were.

When we agreed to write — write until the day came when we were ready to try again — we promised to do so on paper and ink, something we could hold when we couldn't hold each other. I'm holding this paper now like I wish I could hold your hand, but it's not the same.

So, I treasure what I can: the pictures you sent of Nyla growing up, the ones I still have of all of us — the one I carry in my pocket everywhere I go.

When your letters stopped, and I discovered you'd moved on from your address, I didn't know what to do. I looked for you everywhere, but the only place I found you is in my memories. So, I turn to the past instead.

I've gone over that night eight years ago in my mind so many times: could I have done something differently to change it? If I had, would we all still be together again? Other times, I go further — I wake up from dreams where my legs ache from dancing with you, where the music of Miles's Place is at the corner of my mind, just out of reach. It's mine, now — and I spend every day making it sing again.

I go back to our spot all the time. There's a community garden there, and I go at the end of every month. I planted cardamom at first — but it wouldn't take. So instead, I did rows and rows of forget-me-nots — so many that the club decided to change their name in honour of them, and the way each year they surround our little bandstand with blue.

I love my family here, but my family is also you three — my family is everywhere and nowhere. My family is in this letter — this last wish, this answer to a question someone asked me: 'What would you do, if you could write to the love of your past, if there was still a chance?'

Maybe I'll just say this: I love you. Maybe I'll say that if I had one wish, it would be to change time, to make it so it wasn't too late. To have the years back. To be a family again.

Yours, always.

B

8 YEARS   TODAY

8 years ago	Today
is when	I read Dad's letter.
my dad	*Basim*
left.	*left* and came back.

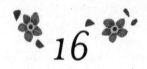

THE ONE TO CHANGE MY LIFE

YOURS, ALWAYS

I put the letter down,
after rereading it
for the fifth time.

My head spins.
Maybe this is a side effect of time-travel:
of having moved somewhere else,
my mind joining another time,
with each word.

Now I'm back here,
and everything feels shaky —
like when you're on the waltzers at the fair
and for a second the whole world tips one way
then holds you in suspension
before jolting you back again.

There are too many questions
turning around in my head:

like why Mum is hiding this from me,
and what it means that
I'm hiding things from her,
like this letter Dad wrote to her.
But if I show her
she might take it — and the truth —
away — might keep it

with all the other secrets
she hid on her phone call.

Questions like how to understand a dad
who carries my picture in his pocket,
but runs away before we come to the door.

Tears dash down my face
like the buttons that fell
from Grandma's box:
scattering over everything.

I look at my own hands in front of me.
They do so much already,
maybe they can do one thing more.
Like take control of finding the truth.
And getting the answers I need
to understand who I am —
who my family is.

I pull out my pen, my notebook,
where the questions once stood
of who 'I Am',
and how to begin a presentation about my dad.
It now hums with the words:
Find him.

Maybe I'll find the version of Dad
whose voice comes out of the letter:
the one who seems to care about me.

Or, maybe, I'll find the version who left us.
I don't know what I'll say to him
if I do.

Either way, I'll find answers.
Either way, the secret that has been hiding
inside my whole life
will no longer be kept from me.

Between my notebook,
my clues,
and my own investigating,
I'm going to be the one to change my life
this time.

LIST OF THINGS THAT CAN TRAVEL THROUGH TIME:

1) Artefacts in museums
2) Archaeologists
3) Fossils
4) Books
5) Letters
6) Grandma
7) Dad's memories
8) Me?

PART 2

CLUES — THE STORY SO FAR

LETTER

Miles's Place — bar? club?
It's his — every day he makes it sing?
Gardening club — he is there once a month?

But where? Our spot? Bandstand with forget-me-nots?
There were more letters to him?
Did he send any back?
Why did he stop?
If he didn't know where we lived
then how come he does now?

Why did he post a letter then run away?
He carries my picture.
What does it mean?

MUM'S PHONE CALL

Hiding something about Dad
Something to change my life?
Mum said: 'I made a promise Nyla wouldn't
have to know this.' Know what?!

He left.
But who was she talking to???

GRANDMA

1) Supermarket sighting
2) House sighting delivering letter
3) Saying he left that night after a big argument
4) Insisting he's not dead — no certificate

Why how? Sister Amina phone call — 2 days
before letter. Has she said something to him?
Does he know I'm looking?

How did he find us? How do I find him?
Will he come back?

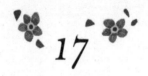

17

BREADCRUMBS

PROJECT UPDATE

In the canteen at lunch,
Jess asks:
'So, what did you discover?'
and I almost jump out of my seat.

'What do you mean?'

'You know, for your history project.
You were gonna use it to find out more
about your dad.
Have you been lurking by the supermarket,
have there been any more sightings
from Grandma Farida's
magic mind?'
Jess laughs,
but I feel my face go pale(ish).

I open my mouth to tell her,
but I don't think I'm ready yet —
how would I even explain it,
how would I know she'd not tell anyone else?
And then another promise
that someone in my family had made
would be broken, but this time,
it would be because of me.

#NOFILTER, OR, THINGS JESS HAS SAID TO MUM WHEN SHE SHOULDN'T

'If Grandma Farida is Nyla's dad's mum, where're your parents?
Are they dead? How? When?'

'My dad bought me a laptop and a tablet and a phone,
you should get one too!'

'My mum always says cheap food is unhealthy,
we like to eat organic.'

'How come you never bake?'

'So, what's it like, having a kid who is mixed?
Do people think Nyla doesn't look like you?
Personally, I really think she does —
I mean, just look at the size of the nose on your face!
Will hers grow that big too?'

BREADCRUMBS

Instead, the information I give to Jess is limited,
breadcrumb-small:
'Well, I found out some stuff about his life,
like where he was born, and where he worked,'

'Oh, yeah, your dad worked in a hospital, right?'

'Yeah, he was a nurse.
And next I want to look into some old ...
memories of places that were important to him.'

This was part of my resolution last night
to follow the clues from the letter,
starting with *Miles's Place* —
the place he says he's at every day.
And, less solid, but still something:
the gardening club.

'What about yours?' I say,
hoping to distract Jess.

'Well.' She leans forward,
her eyes bright.
'Rehearsals have been going so perfectly,
that I was thinking,
I bet there's someone famous in my history,
like maybe my talent is hereditary?
Like we saw with the plants in biology, osmosis,
like maybe it just rubs off my dad
on to me.'

From somewhere within me,
Jess manages to pull a laugh.

'Just imagine if my ancestors were famous,
like a Hollywood star.' Jess tosses her hair
over her shoulder, before saying with a sigh:
'Then maybe I could be too.
Maybe I'd live a really exciting life,
and everyone would love me.'

Maybe I'm not the only one reaching
for something more than myself,
more than my life.
Maybe I'm not the only one with wishes.

'You know, Jess,' I say,
'I can totally see it. I think you must be right.'

AFTER SCHOOL

When I get to the library,
I nearly jump with joy when I see
that the door is finally open.

I rush in, my eyes darting straight to the corner
where Ray and I —

empty.

Our orange and green bean bags sit alone.
There's not even an indentation.
It's as if he was never there.

'It's so lovely to have you back, Nyla!'
Miss Haldi calls, coming over.
'Sorry it took so long —
so much faff over replacing the
alarm you wouldn't believe!
How are you? Is your friend coming?'

I shrink down into myself.
'No.'

Miss Haldi's face is how I imagine a character looks
in my library books
whenever someone says they are 'crestfallen'.

I feel like I'm carrying the weight
of all the library's books on me.
I look at them lined up on the shelves,
and for a moment in my mind
each one of the titles on their spines
is replaced by words from the letter:

Dear R

Yours, always.

B

I remind myself: libraries are for information.
That's what the old librarian told me,
when I first signed up. She said:
'Libraries are about helping you find everything
you need.'

While the library can't help me find my friend —
Yet, a small voice whispers in me —
I have something I need to find even more desperately,
and only a handful of clues so far.
I'm hoping the library can help me.

'Miss Haldi, I need to search for something.'

COMPUTER THREE

The library computers are huge
and ancient.

'I've booked you on computer three,'
Miss Haldi says,
with an apologetic look on her face,
that I understand
as the computer starts making a whirring sound
like it's running out of breath.

So much of Dad's letter feels vague,
like the memories Grandma reaches for sometimes
that then slip through her fingers,
fog-like, ungraspable.

I can't do an online search for a promise,
or for the precise location
of Dad's coat pocket
carrying my picture.
But *Miles's Place*, the gardening club.
These feel solid, like the words
'You are here' on a map.
Except the You is Dad.
And the here —
the here is where I'm going to find him.

So I load up a search engine, and type in: 'Miles's Place'.

The first two results are from New Zealand:
the social media accounts of one Mr Miles Place,
and the third is the work profile of someone
in America looking for a job.
I shrug. Good luck, Mr.

The fourth is a series of apartment blocks
on the other side of the country,
due to be built next year.
Mum and Dad grew up here, up North,
so that can't be right —
plus Miles's Place was from the past,
not the future.

I breathe out a sigh of frustration.
The way Dad said in his letter that he made it 'sing',
how he remembered music and dancing —
I felt like Miles's Place would be somewhere you could go.
But the words take me nowhere.
The computer timer beeps:
my library time is up,
and it's time to get home for Grandma.

There's still the garden, I think.
Tomorrow I'll start there.

I throw my backpack on my shoulder,
and walk through the library doors,
pushing through, straight into —

'Oomph!' I look up,
colliding into someone,
their hand adjusting the round glasses
resting on their concerned face
as we look at each other
and both say at the same time:
'Nyla!' 'Ray!'

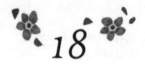

THE SCRAPS IN OUR HANDS

WHAT I WANT TO SAY: ROUND TWO

I want to say   'You're back!'
I want to say   'Are you okay? Are we still friends?'
I want to say   'Did you miss hanging out last week as much as I did?'
I want to say   'I'm sorry if I upset you.'
I want to say   'Did you come here looking for me?'

WHAT WE BOTH SAY IN A BLUR:

'I'm sorry!'

'No, I'm sorry, I shouldn't have—'

'No, I am, it's not your—'

'It's just—'

'It's that—'

We both breathe out a huge puff,
talking over each other in waves.

But when I look at the expression on Ray's face,
something feels different.

'Ray, is everything okay?'

RAY'S GOT SOMETHING TO SAY

'I came last week.
I tried to find you,
but every day it was closed,
and I didn't know what to do,
and I —
I —
I-maybe-made-things-worse-I-don't-know.'

I look at him, confused.
'What's going on?
Why did you run away at the pool —
did I do something?
Did someone say something?
I can help if there's something wrong—?'

My voice comes out strained.
I'm glad we're on the library steps,
and not inside — so no one else can hear.

'I left the pool because I saw something,'
Ray says. 'And I freaked out.
Like majorly FREAKED out,
like, Nyla, you've no idea ...'
Ray pauses, as if realising that he
might be freaking out now, too.
'I didn't know what to do,
it happened so fast —
I suspected when we were looking on my phone,
and then when I saw your notes,
and I couldn't help it,
I turned the page while I was waiting,
and realised—'

My mind races as he talks,
trying to piece things together:
I'd gone away to call Sister Amina,
then come back, and my notebook had been open,
and it had been turned to —
remember —
it had been turned to —

'You saw my drawing of my dad's birth certificate?'

Ray nods.

'But why would that freak you out?' I ask.
It comes out all wobbly and strange.

Ray's whole face looks tense and frantic,
and a feeling of realisation comes over me,
as if I had been picked up from those benches
Ray and I sat on together,
and d
    r
      o
        p
          p
            e
              d
                straight into the pool.

'You know something,' I say.
'You know something about my dad.'

RAY'S MESSAGE

'It's not my story to tell,'
Ray blurts out.

'But I've been searching for him,' I say,
fighting to get my words out evenly
between the clash of *hope* and *please tell me*
warring in my jaw.
'I just want to find the truth,
please, Ray — you have to tell me.'

'I can't, I'm sorry, Nyla,' Ray says,
clutching the sides of his blue raincoat.
I feel too shocked to move.

'I don't understand,' I say,
emotion rattling inside me.
'Is that why you wanted to be friends with me?
Did you know all along?'

'No!' Ray rushes forward,
arm outstretched as if he could keep away
even that thought.
'I love being friends with you,
and the chats we have,
and taking you to the pool.
I swear, I didn't realise until—'

Ray stops, taking a deep breath,
looking directly in my eyes.
'I'm just trying — I always try to do
what's right, but
I know it's not my story to tell,
but I want to help you, too,
and I just don't know what to do
and everything I do just seems to
make things worse.'

He talks with his whole body,
as if he's feeling every single word,
and then slings his backpack from off his shoulder,
unzipping it, and pulling something out.

'Please don't ask me to tell you more.
Just, take this.'
He shoves a scrap of paper
into my hand.
'And look — really *look*.'

We stare at each other,
each of our hands
on the scrap in between us.

Ray's face is urgent as he says to me,
before he walks away:

'I am —
I want to be —
I'll always be

your friend.'

PULLED STRAIGHT OUT OF TIME

'IS EVERYTHING OKAY?'

Miss Haldi stands at the library doors,
concern on her face,
as Ray walks away.

I can't hide
the answer from my eyes
or the quiver at the corner of my mouth.
I quickly hide the paper Ray gave me.

'Did you two have a falling out?' she asks.

My jaw trembles.

'You'll work it out,' Miss Haldi says, tentatively.
'The two of you — you'll be back
on those bean bags before you know it.'

I know it's meant to sound comforting:
but it makes it even worse.

'See you soon, Miss Haldi,'
I murmur. 'I'm glad the library is open again.'

PHOTO

I'm halfway home
before I've walked out all the feelings
bouncing inside me
enough to breathe.
Enough to look
at the piece of paper
Ray gave me.

Except — it's not paper
but a photograph,
torn in half.
In it, there's a child,
sitting with two women,
reaching out and holding the hand,
of someone else
on the other side of the tear in the middle.

The picture shakes in my hands,
as the muddle inside me rises up

        and up
             and up,

until my cheeks are wet,
and my eyes sore.

The people in the picture
are Mum, Grandma and me.

STARE

I can't stop staring.
I must have been maybe two or three.

It's as if Ray reached up
and pulled it straight out of time.

We're standing outside,
and the man just out of reach,
his brown hand reaching,
it has to be —

Dad.

Where did Ray get this?

How did Ray get this?

Why did Ray
— who I didn't know two weeks ago —
have a picture of my family?

RAY KNOWS

Ray knows —   Ray knows —   Ray knows —   Ray knows —
    Ray knows —   Ray knows —   Ray knows —
Ray knows —   Ray knows —   Ray knows —   Ray knows —

What?   Something?   My family?   My dad?

MY FIRST IMPULSE

Is to turn back around and to try,
somehow, to catch up with him.
Or, to run to the swimming pool,
so I can beg him to tell me what he knows,
and how he got this picture,
and ask him why he didn't tell me straight away
and if he knows how to find my dad,
if he knew all along.

Something inside me,
in that place where friendship lives,
threatens to break.

'It's not my story to tell.
Please don't ask me to tell you more.'
That's what Ray said, earlier.
That and —
'I always want to do the right thing.
I'll always be your friend.'

I stand in the street,
looking at the photo in my hand,
tears rolling like marbles
down my face.

NOT A GOOD DAY

It's hard to stay mad at someone
when you're worried about someone else.

I can tell by the look on Maria's face
when she drops Grandma off:
the small lower of Maria's chin,
and shake of her head.
Today is Not a Good Day.

I tuck the picture away.
There's something — someone —
more important than everything else.

When Grandma gets off the bus,
wobbling slightly in her little red coat,
she is moving slowly,
her hands tapping at her pockets
as if she has forgotten something,
her face a frown.

Maria walks her up to the door.
'Tell your mum I'll call her at the end of the week,'
she says to me, and then seems to think better of it.
'Actually, don't worry — I'll text her.'

'Tea time, Grandma,'
I say, trying to keep a spring in my voice,
hoping it'll light a spark in her eyes.
But it's like she's staring
far out into space
and I'm not even sure if she sees me
at all.

I give her her tea:
and she is quiet,
doesn't pick it up,

and her eyes when I hold the cup to her lips
remind me not of her
but of someone smaller,
maybe even myself.

But it's times like this
when my grandma is her wide eyes,
and her dark plait,
and her same warm, wrinkly hands,
but quiet on the inside,
it's these days that are the worst.

Because I miss Grandma,
but more than that,
I worry that the more these days come
the closer I am to the day
that I won't be able to help look after her,
and what happens then?

QUESTIONS IN THE QUIET

In bed that night,
when everyone has gone to sleep,
and the house is quiet,
the occasional Grandma snore through the walls,
I pull the photograph back out of my notebook,
and stare at it.

It feels so strange,
to have a snapshot of an old memory,
of something I was in —
but don't remember.
Sat on Grandma's knee,
Mum beside her,
and my eyes looking back at me now,
my baby hand
wrapped around the finger
of a wide hand,
its owner out of view
right along the tear.

I've never held a photo of me and Dad before.
I've seen them, on Mum's phone,
but this is on paper, in my hands.
I think back to his letter,
about having something physical to hold.

I know what you mean.

And it was Ray
who gave this back to me.
That hurt feeling before suddenly warms
and it makes me even more confused.

At the pool, Ray told me
that he just wanted someone to see him
as he truly was.

And I said: 'Any time.'
I think any time is now,
is the choice that even though I don't understand
why Ray can't tell me,
I know that he's trying to help.

I look at the photo again.
'*Look, really look,*' Ray had said.
But all I see is the three of us,
standing on a random street corner,
and Dad's hand reaching into the frame.

What is Ray trying to show me?
How will this help me find my dad?

20

TIME TO TELL

A FRIEND IN NEED, A FRIEND INDEED

'*Bonjour, chérie!*' Jess says,
when we sit down in the school cafeteria
the next day at lunch.
'I phoned your house
twice last night,
but nobody answered.
I had to practise my lines with the dog!'

'Sorry,' I say, imagining Jess's dog
with a white ruff around his neck,
like the picture of Shakespeare from Jess's play.

'It's okay,' Jess says, and suddenly she looks
like a mirror of me: slightly guilty,
caught up in her thoughts.

And then it all comes out in a spill:
'Is everything okay? Just because
you've been kinda quiet lately
and I was wondering if it was because
I was being such a diva the other day,
and then I thought maybe
I was asking too many questions
after history last week, and if it was, I'm sorry —
Mum says I can be insensitive and I need to think more
about how other people feel before I open my mouth,'
Jess says in one big rush.

I look up at her, and can see the worry in her expression.
How would it feel, to tell Jess the truth?
Not just about my search,
to find my dad, or Ray,
to ask what he wanted me to see in the photograph —
but about those questions.
About how it made me feel, too.

'Jess ...' I say, hesitantly.

'Oh, shiz,
you look serious,
it *is* about history, isn't it?
I knew I was too pushy — your family
are yours and I'm so sorry if I made you feel like
you had to be Miss Zimbabwean History when I should have
just been your friend and listened to how
that lesson made you feel and—'

'Jess!' I say.
'You know, if you're apologising,
you should let the other person speak, right?'

'I'm sorry!' Jess says, closing her lips tight,
but as she meets my eyes hers are open,
her bouncing body slowing down to a listening still.

'Okay, so, yeah — it did make me feel kinda weird.
Like you weren't seeing me as Nyla,
but as, like — I dunno —
someone to be looked at from the outside,
when usually we always talk from the inside.
From each other. As friends.'

Jess nods, a gentle quiet
in the wide-open space around us,
and we both sit in it — reflecting on my words.
I think about how our conversation feels brave.

'Thank you for telling me,' Jess says,
after a while.
'And sorry for, you know—'

'An avalanche apology?'

'Not giving you space to speak.'

I lean into her,
my head on her shoulder.

'Thanks for thinking
about this stuff,' I say.
'And me.'

Jess nods against me.
'Do you think we can always try to be
the friends who talk about stuff,
even when shiz gets tough
and we don't know what to do?'
she asks.

'I hope so,' I say,
linking my arm through hers,
and as I do, I think of Ray with a pang,
of a million different notes, the loudest one
being wanting to share that promise with him, too.

'It's not always easy to know
what the right thing to do is, is it?'
I say.

Jess nods. 'It's not.
Though, if there's one thing I've learned
from my time on *Hamlet*,
it's that the right thing to do is
rarely to hide behind something called an arras.
That kinda behaviour
will really come back to bite you in the bum.'

WE LAUGH UNTIL IT'S QUIET

We laugh until it's quiet,
and in the quiet,
something rises,
like a small kernel of trust.

'*Is* everything okay, though?'
Jess asks, gently.
'Like, with you?'

I take a deep breath.
'Jess, can you keep a secret?'

Jess turns to me,
her face a mix of excitement
and seriousness.

'I swear on my dubious-yet-potential-Hollywood-ancestry
that I will keep secret whatever you are about to tell me.'
And then she looks around,
to check that no one is listening,
before adding in a whisper:
'Lay it on me, Elachi.
I'm ready.'

I TELL JESS EVERYTHING

I tell her about the missing death certificate,
and Grandma saying she saw my dad, again,
and the letter on the doorstep
— *'No. Actual. Way!' she says* —
and Grandma making me promise to keep it a secret
but asking me to find him
— *'Grandma Farida!'* —
and Mum's phone call I overheard
— *'Holy mothballs and a half!'* —
about something which 'could change my life'.

I tell her about Miles's Place and the gardening club
and the clues all written down in my notebook,
and Ray
— *'Wait, slow down, I need details,*
age, hobbies, star sign' —
and the photograph and questions mounting up
and secrets swirling round
faster than I can count.

When I'm done,
Jess sits back, and strokes her chin
as if stroking an imaginary beard.
'HmmmmmmmmmmMMMMMMMMmmmmm,'
she says.

'I know.'

'This is, like,' she says, 'a lot.
Like there's more drama than my play,
and that's saying something.'

'Yeah, but unlike your play,
there's no script for this.
I don't know what to do next.'

'HmmmMMMMmmm,' Jess says again,
then suddenly sits forward,
pulling her phone out of her pocket.
'Well, you've come to the right place, *chérie*,
because like any detective's assistant,
I know exactly where you need to begin.
You're a smart cookie, sweet Nyla,
but it's gonna take more than a search engine
to crumble this cake—'

'What are you on about?'

'The power of social media!
That's what we need
to crack this case like a nut. BOOM!
Let's do it.'

'Okay, but remember, it's a secret,'
I say, convinced she's going to put a post
on her social media telling everyone.

'What do you take me for? A rookie?
I'm not going to tell anyone —
but what I'm thinking is,
if we can track down some of the people
in this mystery plot of yours online,
maybe we can find out more about them.'
A mischievous look spreads over her already mischievous face.
'Let's try and draw these suspects
out of hiding, shall we?'

SEARCH

Jess offers me the phone,
but I shake my head —
I felt excited when searching on Ray's phone,
but now I'm so nervous my knees are shaking the table
(Jess's raised eyebrow says she's noticed that, too).

Jess opens the app
that most kids in my school use
(and most adults, too).
Mum says I can't have an account until I'm older,
she says she doesn't want me to see something I shouldn't,
or meet someone who isn't who they say they are.
Or discover what you've been hiding, I wonder.
Then I feel guilty. I'm hiding things from her, too.

'How about we start with Ray?' Jess suggests.
'Or *maybe* you should just go to the pool —
stage a surprise?'

'No. The pool's his favourite place,
and he asked me not to ask him for more information.
It wouldn't feel right.' I pause.
'It would feel like breaking a promise.'

Jess hmms, and looks at me, patiently.

'I can search for anyone, right?' I ask.

'Sure, if they have a profile.'

I hesitate. Why not just go straight
to the source?

'My dad. Basim Elachi,' I say.
It feels so strange
saying his name out loud.

'One Basim Elachi coming up,'
Jess whispers as she types his name in;
her voice is softer, as if she knows
how significant this is.

Both of us hold our breath.

BLANK SPACE

Nothing.
Not a mention
not a line
no Basim
no Elachi
nothing.

'That's weird,' Jess says.
'Most people my parents' age have this app, too.
Or have at least been mentioned once,
like, look—'
and she types in her mum's name,
showing her profile,
and all the times her name
has been mentioned in other people's comments.

'Do you think that's, like, a sign?
Like it was deliberately removed?'
I ask.

Jess shrugs.
'A cover-up is one option.
But also, not everyone is on social media.
I'm sorry, Nyla.'

I grit my teeth.
There's something I'm not getting at,
some thread that I need to pull
that would lead me to the right answer
if only I can figure out
the right question.

Wait.

'Jess, could you try one more name for me?'

I SEE SOMEONE I SHOULDN'T

'Can you try searching "Amina Brown"?'
Even as I ask,
I feel scared of what I might see.

A list of profiles comes up:

Amina Brown Landscape Architect
Amina Brown Catering
Amina Brown — HDG

'HDG,' I say, and Jess clicks.

'It's private. Does that mean we can't see anything?'

Jess scrolls down,
the words 'Add friend' blocking any further content.
'In theory, yes, but do not worry, *mon amie*,
my older cousin taught me how to snoop!'
and Jess clicks on Amina's profile picture,
and starts swiping through it,
revealing picture after picture.

'Profile pictures are always public,'
Jess explains, and then,
'Oh, wait — isn't that ...?'
And her voice trails off,
to a selfie of Sister Amina,
a baby in her arms,
and cheek to cheek
with a man with curly hair,
a man who looks just
like
me.

'My dad.'

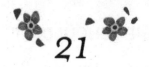

21

A HAND, A HUG, A WORD

'WHEN WAS THIS TAKEN?'

I ask, and Jess taps the phone,
scrolls forward and back.
'I don't know —
she had it as her picture seven years ago.'
AKA after-Dad-disappeared-out-of-my-life.
'But it doesn't say *when*.
Like, anybody could have any profile picture
from any time *at* any time.'

Jess sounds slightly frantic,
almost tense — as if she's thinking
the exact same thing as me.
'Do you want me to add her as a friend,
maybe conduct my own intervie—'

'No!' I say, quickly,
remembering how definite Amina's voice was
on the phone.

Jess and I go back to staring at the picture.

'They look really close,'
Jess says.

There's a curdling, sinking feeling in my gut,
made worse by the fact that right about now,
Jess would usually be saying the worst thing she could,
like:
'OMG, do you think they were having an affair?'
Or,
'WAIT! Do you think she's his secret lover?'

But she doesn't.

She just looks at me with that same emotion on her face,
that I've run from a thousand times already,
as if she knows not to say it,
not to ask if there's more to what we are both thinking.

CONCLUSIONS ARE DRAWN LIKE SWORDS

I shove up from the table,
leaving Jess staring after me
as I walk away,
every inch of my body filled with rage.

I knew Sister Amina was hiding something —
and it looks like a pretty big something:
my dad holding a baby with her
when he wasn't there for me.

Everything soft in me suddenly rolls into hard.

'Nyla!' I hear Jess's voice,
but it sounds so far away from me
that my head doesn't even turn
as I stomp out of the canteen,
out of the school.

The anger that I'd kept caged up
— squashed it down as it paced against my ribs —
rises until it's all I can see.
And its name is not Dad,
or Amina, or Mum.
Its name is Nyla — me.

Angry at everyone else
for lying,
and angry at me
for believing it all,
for reading that letter from my dad,
the line: *I want us to be a family again*,
and thinking
that maybe
if I found him

we could be.

A HAND, A HUG, A WORD

'Nyla!' Jess is breathless when she catches up with me.
I'm in the middle of the school field,
walking directionless, kicking up chunks of mud.

Other kids are looking,
but I don't care.

'I know how it looks,' Jess says.

'Yeah, it looks like my dad
was having it off with someone else!'
I shout, but the words feel so wrong in my mouth.
They don't feel like me.

'Yeaaaahh, maybe, buuuuttt,' Jess draws out,
and then stops me still, holding my shoulders,
looking straight into my face.
'Look, I'm the first to go into the full dramatics,'
Jess says, gently trying to tug at the corners of my frown.
'But all you've seen is a picture.
And, didn't you tell me, I dunno,
didn't you say that this was about chasing facts,
and you trying to find out the truth?'

Jess's words sink in slowly.

'I get why you're mad,' she says, 'and if it is true,
I'll put off my plans to go vegan like other celebrities
and we can egg the homes of all your enemies,
but, until then — maybe — I don't know —
my dad always says that you should give people a chance,
and not judge the situation
before you know the full facts—?
Like, yeah, okay, the picture doesn't look great,
but, like — couldn't it be — I dunno — don't you think you should
try and find out first, before jumping to this —
admittedly super plausible — conclusion?'

I look down at the ground,
the last of the rage stamping itself out,
in the kick of my shoe against a stone.

'It's just—' I begin,
but don't know how to explain
spending my whole life missing someone,
and reading the letter, thinking they miss me
and then seeing a picture of them with someone else,
wondering what if —
what if they had another family?

I look at Jess,
as if my face could explain it all,
and she grabs me,
and wraps me in a hug.

'We'll figure it out,' she says.
'You're not alone.'

I hug her back,
and imagine I'm hugging
that hurt
angry
part of me,
too.

ONE LAST QUESTION

The lunch bell goes,
and we walk back to class.

'Jess?' I ask.

'Yes, *chérie?*' she replies.

'Where did you learn the word "plausible"?'

22

ALL ROADS LEAD TO HILLWORTH

ONE LAST LOOK

When I get to the library that afternoon,
I only glance at the bookshelves
before heading straight to the computers.

Miss Haldi is at the front desk,
her head bent over pages,
a pen in the corner of her mouth.
When I walk up to her,
she looks like she's about
to pick up where we left off yesterday —

I jump in instead.
'Can I go on the computers again?'

YOUR SEARCH HERE: _____

I look in my notebook,
at the parts of Dad's letter that I copied down:
the parts about a garden with a bandstand
surrounded by forget-me-nots,
and a club that changed its name
to honour them.
I type each letter into the browser
with purpose.
Each one significant,
determined,
knowing the power of where a full sentence can lead:
to a page full of possibilities.

'Bandstand + Community Garden + Forget-Me-Not Club'

I find it three listings down.

A homemade website:
Forget-Me-Not Community Garden
— word omitted: bandstand —
but, instead, underneath it,
another word like a beacon:
Hillworth.

ALL ROADS LEAD TO HILLWORTH

I don't remember Hillworth much.
It's where I was born,
where Mum and Dad grew up,
where Grandma lived
when she first came to the UK.

When I couldn't find Miles's Place listed,
I'd thought maybe I'd gotten it wrong.
Maybe the special place — 'our spot' — wasn't in Hillworth,
after all.

But the community garden,
in the same town where this all began.
Where my family, my parents,
first started out—?

Some things aren't coincidence.

WWW.FORGETMENOTGARDENCLUB.COM

The text is slightly jumbled up,
like there's a fault in the code
that no one has noticed yet.

I start looking for pictures first,
but there's no people in them,
only flowers.
In the background of some
there's a blurry wooden bandstand,
white paint peeling —
That's it! That has to be it!

I scroll down as fast as I can,
trying to find more details.
It says the club is run by people
from all over the community, who take care of it.
At the bottom there's a list of things
they've raised funds for,
by selling seeds and flowers,
and it's not organisations or charities,
but people:

Mohamed Family Hajj
Mike's boiler repair
Fixed Artie's roof!
Hillworth High Free School Uniforms

And at the bottom
there's a small button:

Contact Us

BE SMART

Okay, I need to think.
Dad's letter said he goes there once a month.
It has to be here — Hillworth, bandstand, forget-me-nots.
I feel giddy, like I'm on a train speeding so fast,
I can't get off.

I'm close.
I need to find where exactly in Hillworth it is.
I click on the 'Contact Us' page,
and in the small box to enter my message
I type:

Hi! My dad is part of your club

No, wait, that's too obvious,
and I don't want him to know I'm looking for him yet,
not without having found him for sure first —

Hi! My dad would like to join your gardening club

But then why wouldn't he just email himself?

Hi! I'd like to join your club. Where do you meet?
Do you have a list of times when it's free, as I am very busy?

It needs to sound genuine,
so I add at the end:
Kind regards
because that's what emails
written by adults are signed off with,
I think.

Hmm. I need to leave an email address
for them to reply to — and if I leave my school one,
they'll know it's me, it says my name.

Instead, I use
the only other email address
I know by heart.

I hope Jess doesn't mind.

PRACTISING LINES

That night,
when I get home,
my mind ticks and tocks, wondering
if the club will even read my email
or ever get back to me.

I phone Jess before bed and give her a heads-up
about using her email address.
'*Mais oui, mon amie,*
I can be both detective's assistant
and a budding young star.
It's classic Gemini,
after all.'

'Remember, it's a secret,' I whisper,
before I put her on speaker
and we rehearse her lines
with Grandma,
who has been in one of those moods
where every time I ask her a question,
she replies by singing.

'Grandma, do you know about a bandstand,
that Mum and Dad went to in Hillworth?
Do you know why he left?'

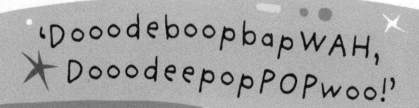

'DooodeboopbapWAH,
DooodeepopPOPwoo!'

'Grandma, do you know
a boy called Raymond?'

'Dooodeepop POPwoo,
Dooodeboopbap WAH!'

When Mum gets home she is quiet,
for once both of us more lost in our thoughts
than Grandma.

I think about telling Mum —
but when so much has been kept from me already,
the only way to know the truth
is to find it myself.

I'm going to find you, Dad, I think,
sending up my thoughts
to the sky.
I'm getting closer — whether you did run away,
or whether there was some other reason
you couldn't — didn't —
stay.

23

B.E. MARKS THE SPOT

INFORMATION TECHNOLOGY

It takes until Thursday,
before the gardening club replies.

First period, in IT,
Jess whispers from her computer to me:
'Okay, I got this email at ridiculous-o-clock
this morning, like, 6 a.m. Seriously, who is up then?'
We both keep our eyes on the supply teacher,
talking at the front of the class.
I hope she can't hear us whispering.
'I haven't read it. I didn't think you'd want me to
see what it says before you, and
frankly, Nyla, for that I deserve a medal.'

I slide my chair closer to hers,
as the teacher tells us to do something
on a spreadsheet, something about using a formula
to add numbers quickly.

'Do you need help?' she calls to us,
and Jess replies cheerily,

'No! I'm just showing Nyla how.'

I nudge her. 'Why can't it be me showing you?'

'True,' Jess says, and then leans over
as if ready to shout to the teacher,
before laughing as I nudge her back,
and we turn to the screen:

'Thank you for asking about our club,
we always love having new members!'
Jess whispers, reading the email out loud.
'Please see attached our rota — oh, yeah,
there's something attached here,
cool — *for signs of our busiest times.*
I'm sure any of our members
would love to introduce you
to the garden. We're located
by the bandstand
in Greenwood Park.'

My heart thrums in my chest.
Greenwood Park — a solid place.

Jess and I glance at the teacher,
before I whisper:
'Open it, now!'

She does,
but then the teacher comes over:
'Girls, I want to see proof
that you're working
on your formulas.'

'We are!' Jess trills. 'In fact,
would it be okay if we print this one out?'

The teacher grumbles,
and waves a hand as if to say 'If you must.'

I rush to the printer,
hoping no one else sees
that the only formulas we're printing
are the ones to solve not numbers
but the riddle
of my own family.

FORGET-ME-NOT ROTA

In English, between the pages
of the anthology we're reading,
I slide out the printout of the rota
from the gardening club.
Forget-Me-Not Rota,
it reads at the top.
Don't forget your slot!

The rota is a puzzle in itself,
no specific dates just:
'First Monday morning of the month'
and 'Second Tuesday afternoon of the month'
and on and on.
Underneath each is a list of initials.
Some days are full —
Sundays in particular.

I flick through,
looking at the initials,
trying to recognise anything that looks familiar —
first week, nothing,
second week, nothing,
third week, nothing,
fourth week—

and there,
on the third to last day
of the final week of the month,
a set of initials
that halt me in my tracks:

B.E.

B.E. MARKS THE SPOT

The initials marked in a garden slot
jump out at me on the page,
a flashing, blinking beacon.

My finger shakes as I trace it up the rota,
until I find the time they belong to:

AM: *Last Friday of the Month.*

My dad's letter echoes in my head:
'*I go at the end of every month.*'

My heart beats fast
as I pull my school planner out of my bag,
flick through the weeks until:
tomorrow.

The last Friday of the month
is
<u>tomorrow</u>.

BELL

The bell rings for the end of school.
As we shove our things in our bags,
I can't wait to tell Jess what I found —
how tomorrow is my chance to find my dad!

I go over to her,
but our English teacher gets there first
and says:
'I'll be coming along tomorrow, Jess.
Good luck, I can't wait!'

As we amble out of the class,
I link my arm through Jess's:
'What did Miss mean —
where is she coming?'

'The dress rehearsal, of course, baby!
We're doing it early because Ms Mills said
she got a good deal on the costumes.
Don't tell me you've forgotten again?'

'Of course not!'
The lie that comes out of my mouth
is so small, so easy.

Jess asks me if I found anything on the rota
but all my words, my realisation,
fall behind that lie in my mouth:
'Nothing.'

Jess frowns slightly,
like there's something more she wants to say.
Instead, she gives me a hug,
as we head off our separate ways home
across the school field.

At the back of my mind,
two threads pull:
Keep my promise to Jess and go to her rehearsal
or
Find my dad.

DECISION TIME

If I don't go
1)   I get to watch Jess's rehearsal and cheer her on
2)   I have to wait another month before I can try to find my dad
3)   I have more time to prepare — how do I even get to Greenwood Park?

If I go tomorrow
1)   How will I get off school, to get there early enough to try and catch him?
2)   What if he's not there, what if the rota/the initials aren't right?
3)   Will Jess forgive me — should I tell her I can't come?
4)   If I go, I don't have to wait another month — I can't wait that long, what if the secret runs away from me? I can't keep hiding it from Mum.
5)   If I go tomorrow, then I can finally find the answers about my dad.

And with that my decision is made.

24

MY THOUGHTS CHASE ME

PREPARATIONS

On my way home from school,
I run into the library.
'Miss Haldi — is there a computer free?'

She waves a yes from the corner,
where she's half snowed under
a pile of books marked 'Urgent Request'.

'Can I print something out too?' I ask,
and I hear a small 'Please do!'
called from where she is hidden.

On the computer,
I print a map to take me from where I live
all the way to Greenwood Park in Hillworth,
and back.
It brings up a picture of a dotted route.
The X5. Of course.

I trace my finger from where I know —
the supermarket, the pool —
to where I don't —
beyond. Hillworth.

As I rush out of the library,
Miss Haldi comes up behind me,
catching me just as I'm outside the door.
'Did you make up with your friend?'

I shake my head. 'No. Not yet.'

'I'm sorry to hear it.' She pauses,
then says, suddenly slightly shy:
'I'm having a book clear-out at home,
and I thought some may be of interest to you.
There're some real gems:
one of my favourite anthologies of Muslim women's writing,
some great poetry and fantasy and
there's several in there too about being,
you know.
Like us.
Mixed.'

I look at her.
'You're mixed?'

She nods excitedly.
'I heard you and your friend, Ray,
talking the other day.
I'd be happy to loan some of mine to you?
Maybe you could even use them
as a peace offering with him?'

If my feelings were like Grandma's button box,
they'd be a mix of ones that are curious, and sad.

'I could bring them in, or drop them off
next time I see my wee window waver?' she offers.

It feels like the smallest,
biggest kindness.

'Thank you,' I say.

ON MY WAY

As I head down the library steps,
my button-box feelings dance in my mind:
Greenwood Park — Bus Timetable —
Miss Haldi Bringing Books.
One feels like *hope*
one feels like *action*
one feels something like *care*,
something like *hug*.
I wrap them all around me,
hitch my backpack slightly higher on my back
as I walk past the newsagent's.
I'm smiling as I think
about the books Miss Haldi talked about,
and how tomorrow
I could finally piece together the mystery,
until a hand comes clipping
round the back of my head.

JUST WHEN YOU THINK YOU'RE ON THE HOME STRAIGHT

'Look at you, geek!' comes the shout,
and I realise he's there, again
just like he was before —
Harry.
He must have seen me
when he was coming out of the newsagent's,
or what if he'd been waiting for me outside the library?
My eyes widen and my pulse quickens its pace.

'Hanging in the library again, I see,'
Harry says, while I try to dodge away, ear stinging.
'Don't you know it's not safe for the books with you in there?
Pants On Fire might burn the whole place down!'

I feel so far away from safety
and Miss Haldi.
Harry pushes my shoulders
and with it pushes out all other thoughts.
H
   o
      p
         e
       A
     c
   t
     i
       o
         n
        C
     a
  r
e

spiralling down to my feet.

And there, on the ground,
snags the smallest thought,
Harry's words echoing around me:
Pants On Fire might burn the whole place down.

'It was you!' I am surprised by the shout
of my own voice as I look up.
'You smashed the library fire alarm!
You were the reason the library had to close.'

Harry grins,
and every inch of his teeth
feels sharp and hard.

I try to push forward, past him;
he just walks backwards
at pace with me,
his face in my face.

'I don't know what you mean,'
he says —

   step forward,

      step back —

'And even if I did —
you can't prove anything,'
and then his smile goes even wider,
until I feel like I'm in the jaws of a shark,
'or stop it happening again.'

The truth is a curdle of fear lodged deep in my gut.
'I won't let you,' I start,
and though my voice feels small,
it's there. 'I'll tell—'

'Tell who? That librarian?'
His laugh is followed by a mocking sneer.
'You're mixed too oh blah blah blah,'
Harry says in a sing-song voice,
every inch of him a jeer.
'Has she changed your library card yet,
to Nyla Pants On Fire?'

My face burns. *He's been listening to us.*
He laughs again,
his breath hot as a furnace.

Leave me alone
are all my thoughts say,
and,

        Go,

            Go,

                Go!

                But I remember my conversation with Jess,
                  after the last time Harry came by.
            'He doesn't get to decide what my name means.'
          And I remember, too
          talking with Ray,
          how brave he is,
          and his uncle's tales,
          and how when you stand up for yourself —
          you're standing up for a whole lot more, too.
And I think of the library,
of all the books —
of the safe place,
and Miss Haldi's face.

No.
No.

'Don't you have something better to do
than to make fun of people's names?'

My voice comes out so strong
so clear
it's like it's under its own spell.

'It's not okay, Harry. My name is brilliant,
and you making fun of it—'
my courage shakes

but something pushes me through,
'it's racist.'

Harry draws his lips back,
repulsed.
'You can't call me that!' he says.

He pushes his face so close
that I can see the spittle
wobbling between his teeth.

'Besides,' he says,
the meanest of mean looks in his eye,
his voice a low hiss of steam.
'How can it be racist
when you're only half a thing?'

I am all shake,
all quake.

'Do you know what you'll find in those
"mixed books"?'
Miss Haldi's words in his mouth
are as much of a punch as his hands against me,
as he shoves my shoulders.
'Puhhleaaase. Face it,
Pants On Fire, you're only half one of us ...'
Another shove against my shoulders,
His hands hard like hate —
'... and half one of *them*.
You're not even a whole thing.
You're *nothing*.'

He spits,
a white glob landing on my shoes.
I feel so stunned
that I don't move.

Something in his eyes
goes from slits of hard blue,
to conflicted, slightly wider,
as he looks over my shoulder,
eyes widening even more,
at whatever he sees.

I take my chance while he is distracted,
taking everything he's just said
everything he's pushing into my space
and with my voice
shove it back on to him.

My shout is like a gust of the strongest wind,
blowing his fire away:
'My name is Nyla Elachi!'

Harry staggers back,
arms reeling,
almost falling to the ground.

And then,
I run.

AS I RUN, MY THOUGHTS CHASE ME AND THEY SAY:

Nothing – nothing.

NOTHING

This word, it follows me.
It follows me all the way home.

A CONSTELLATION OF NYLA

WHEN

When Maria drops Grandma off,
and asks gently how I am,
I don't smile.

When Grandma holds my two hands in hers,
shifts her hips one way, then the other,
as if asking to dance,
I hold on tight,
but don't smile.

I count out her medicines,
slam down the water so hard on the side
that it flops out, and then hold it so gently
to her mouth, to help her swallow
her pills down.

'There, there.'
 Good.

I give her her fidget blanket,
the one Maria crocheted for her,
sit on the floor by Grandma's feet,
and wonder what it means,
to be called 'half a thing',
to be deemed 'nothing'.

MIXED (VERB)

If being mixed is a verb, a 'doing word',
instead of a noun given to me to hold,
it would be a journey from wanting:
wanting to know, feel, be, understand who I am,

and owning, being all of those things,
defining it for myself.

I know that, deep down inside me,
I don't need anyone else to tell me who I am,
or can be.
I know there's strength in me being me.

But, it's how I cross that bridge,
between noun and verb.

Between something someone else calls you,
and a living word.

How do I be myself,
when it feels like everyone else
has something to say about me?

And how do I know who I am,
without knowing my dad,
and what happened in my family?

Why he left us alone
but still carries my picture
in his coat.

TOO MUCH

I put my face in my hands,
my breath coming out shaky,
until all of the words —
Harry's hard ones,
Miss Haldi's gentle ones,
flood through me.
Despite all the secrets we've been keeping,
I wish that Mum was here.
My face pushes further into my hands,
my body starting to shake
as I feel tears coming —

AND THEN

I feel a pressure,
gentle on the crown of my head
moving down to the nape of my neck.
One. Two.
Grandma's hand moves so slowly.
Stroking my hair.
And although she's the time-traveller,
it is me who had forgotten —
amid the pills and the drop-off
and popping her in her chair —
that she, my grandma, might be far away,
but she is still my grandma.
Hand stroking my hair,
she is still there.

THIS TIME, IN MY NOTEBOOK I WRITE:

My mix is multiples,
a galaxy of stars,
each one a person,
like Mum, Dad, Grandma,
who passed something down
maybe their love, maybe their laugh,
maybe their hand on my head,
comforting and warm.
That I am exactly, fully myself —
a constellation of Nyla,
full of dream swirls and bright sparks.
Not nothing, but everything.
Not half.
Whole.

26

BEYOND

THE NEXT MORNING

I get up early,
before anyone can see me,
before Mum — one hand ready to reach for her alarm
at 5.30 —
before Grandma,
fast asleep and memory-magic dreaming,
before the sun, even.
I sneak downstairs,
find where Mum leaves her phone charging in the kitchen,
and unplug it.
When I tread back up the stairs,
my dressing-gown pocket is heavier.
I feel guilty,
but I have no time to waste.

THE PLAN IN MOTION

I cough.
'Oh, no, Mum. I really don't feel well at all.'
Pull the covers up over my face
(can't let my expression give me away).

'Nyla, get out of bed. You're going to be late for school.'

'I can't, Mum. I'm sick.'
I cough again.

'What are you feeling? Have you seen
my phone? I'm going to be late for work.'

Cough. Cough. Cough.
I feel cool hands
against my face.

'Hmm. Your temperature is okay.
Should I stay home? Are—'

'No! I mean, I think it's just something mild,
but better that I rest.'

'I don't like the idea of leaving you on your own.'

'It's just a cold, Mum.
Didn't you say you're going to be late?'

'Okay. I'll call school from work,
tell them you won't be in. If you get worse,
call me on work's number if you need me, okay?'

'Don't worry, Mum —
I'll probably just sleep it off.'

She nods, a worried frown,
before a noise comes from downstairs.
'That's Grandma's bus at the door
— sorry I can't stay, love.
Feel better soon.'

Hidden under the covers,
I clench Mum's mobile phone
tight in one hand,
my guilt in the other.

BEYOND

I dress in my school uniform
with a hoody over the top
in case I get caught out.
That way I can say
I'm on my way to an appointment
or got sent home early.

Dad's letter is tucked into my bag
like a talisman, alongside the maps from the library,
Mum's phone as back-up,
my notebook, and a bag of crisps.

When I get on the X5 bus,
it's just me,
and two old ladies with their shopping trolleys,
calling to each other with laughter
from either side of the bus.
It makes me think of Grandma.

I follow along on my printout map.
It feels comforting, like the paper and ink
Dad spoke about in his letter.
And Ray's photograph.
Things you can touch feel more real.

We pass familiar stops,
the big supermarket,
the pool —
and I can't help but look for Ray at the entrance,
even though I know he won't be there.

But then, the bus drives on,
and I travel beyond where I know until —

SOMEWHERE NEW (AND OLD)

I feel lost. Nothing seems to match:
the view outside the window
with the paper map,
the bus speeding along.

I pull up the map app on Mum's phone —
and I see myself, a blue dot,
wavering and stalling on a yellow road.
Didn't we pass that road it says I'm on
five minutes ago?
The bus takes a swerve around a corner,
and the dot jitters, trying to catch up.

The streets we pass by are all lined with trees:
not like the streets in my area at all.

The houses have changed,
they're not concrete and pebbledash,
but tall, with white sandy stones,
shining like the holiday homes on TV.

The old ladies got off a long time ago,
now it is all mums in posh clothes,
wearing wellies up to their knees.

My mum never dresses like that.

A lady gets on dressed entirely in pink.
She carries a small dog that sits in her lap.
It looks at me and barks:
YAP-YAP-YAP-YAP.

The woman turns and looks at me too
and her eyes say everything in the dog's bark:
We-Don't-Trust-You.

I don't know where I am.
I don't know who to ask.

The woman's eyes keep staring,
and the dog keeps shouting its *YAP-YAP-YAP*
and the mums are cooing their 'jahs' and their 'supers'
and I miss the old ladies with their shopping trolleys
and accents that sound like —

home.

HOME IS A WORD THAT IS A MAGIC SPELL

I remember why I'm here.
Why I wanted to be brave.

I press the bell.
As the bus comes to a stop,
I peer up at the driver.
My voice feels quiet but still I say:
'Are we close to Greenwood Park?
Are we in Hillworth?'

The bus driver smiles.
'Just coming into it now, love.
When we get to Greenwood,
I'll shout for you to get off.'

'Yes, please!' I sit back down,
closer to the front so I can hear him.

Behind me, the dog yap yaps on,
and though I can't see the woman's disapproving eyes
I can feel them.

BORDERLAND

The bus stops, and I get off outside a leafy park
with huge, iron gates.

It's weird —
on the way in to Hillworth the houses were all posh and smart
and then after a while
they were closer to mine again.

I look at the park,
and it's like it's in the middle of all this mix:
all the houses on the right of it
with huge windows, and steps leading up to them.

And on the left, blocks of flats in the distance
watching over me.

I know for a fact
that we would have never lived in the fancy stone ones,
but I wonder if this is where Dad lives now:
if maybe he swapped us for this as well.

Don't judge before you know,
Jess's voice comes back to me,
and I check the time on Mum's phone.
Jess will have realised I'm not at school by now,
and maybe know I'm not coming to rehearsal.

I'm sorry, I whisper to Jess, and to Mum,
as I push through the park gates.

PROMISES TINGED WITH BLUE

AM I A TIME-TRAVELLER, TOO?

As I walk through the park
something in it feels — familiar.
Like I've been here before.
I recognise this place,
as if I'm looking at it,
its long, curved paths,
wide grass verges,
and tall trees,
saying: *I remember you.*
And it's looking at me,
saying:
Welcome back.

In the distance,
I see a white steeple peeking over the top of trees
further ahead in the park.
The bandstand?

I run my hands on my trousers,
my palms all clammy, fingers shaky.
What if I'm finally about to find my dad?

A man walks towards me,
two circles of red on his white cheeks,
pushing a wheelbarrow piled high
with a shovel and soil.

'Excuse me,' I say, breathless,
'is this the way to the community garden?'

'Sure is,' he says, and pauses,
to look back in the direction of the white steeple.
'I've just passed there.
I do the maintenance for the whole park.'

My nervous mouth takes over,
the question jumping out of my mouth
before a second thought:
'Was there, was there a man there,
by any chance? A man who looked like ...
me?'

He turns his head,
looks at me quizzically.
'Aye, maybe. I'm not one
to like to say.'

Part of me is confused at first,
and then I realise he's talking about race.
Typical, I think, and Ray's face
comes to my mind,
rolling his eyes.

I push the wheelbarrow guy's stare
away, as I nod
and carry on up the hill.

FORGET-ME-NOT

I see the bandstand up ahead,
a white wooden hexagon
with steps at the front,
and before those:
flowers.
Rows and rows of blue flowers
and plants of different types,
some wrapped around sticks holding up netting covers
and some sections fresh soil,
as if someone has just planted something
and is waiting for it to grow.

This is it! I think,
and my heart leaps.
All my investigating has brought me here
to the place from the letters
and a place from my family's past.

'Dad?' I call,
moving around the bandstand,
careful not to traipse on the flowers.
'Dad, B—Basim?
Basim Elachi?'

But there's no one there
to reply.

I TELL MYSELF:

It's okay. Yes,
you came all this way.
Yes, you skipped school
and stole Mum's phone
and let down Jess. Again.
But even if your insides feel tangled and heavy,
and even if you suddenly feel afraid
being so far from home —
it's okay.
It's gonna be okay.

GOING ROUND IN CIRCLES

I walk around the bandstand twice,
as if hoping Dad will suddenly appear.
But it's quiet.

The community garden
circles the entire bandstand
like someone started small
and over the years it got bigger and bigger.
I throw myself down on the wooden steps
with a hard, solid *thunk*.
It's not yet lunchtime,
and the rota said Friday morning.
Unless I was wrong,
about the initials, B.E.;
unless I'm in the wrong place?

I run my fingers up and down the grooves of the steps,
trying to calm myself,
realising I've been biting my cheeks.
My fingers run over solid wood,
the railing sturdy.
There's a groove in one
that's deeper than the others,
a swirled indent,
and I trace it again and again,
the movement comforting,
two sides at a diagonal,
meeting two curves on top —

Wait, what?

I lean over, quickly,
and see carved into the wood,
the shape of a heart.
And inside it:
a pair of initials
as familiar
as my own.

B&R

It is like touching an artefact.
Like discovering an ancient treasure
untouched from long ago.
Hidden, facing the bandstand,
on the back of one of the wooden railings,
so small, and so out of the way,
that you'd only find it if you were looking for it.
A heart, carved into the wood,
and inside it:
B&R.

Mum and Dad's special place.
I was right.

As I run my fingers over it,
I imagine my dad carving this heart,
and feel like I am meeting him in this touch.

Feel like this is the closest I've come to him.
To *real*.

I look at the plants around me,
as if they have the answer
of what to do next,
but they just sway slightly in the wind,
the blue petals of forget-me-nots
blowing towards me,
as if this is all I have,
after everything:

a memory carved in wood,
and blue-tinged promises
scattered on the breeze.

I pick one of the forget-me-nots,
its stem soft in my hand.
I hold it close,
as if it could tell me where to go.

'HEY, KID!'

The shout draws me out, and
I look up from where I sit.
Wheelbarrow Guy is back.
He's staring at me, frowning,
his walkie talkie held up
to his mouth.

I know what that look means.

'Are you sure you should be messing around in there?'
Wheelbarrow Guy says, starting towards me.

One of Grandma's swear words
in a language I don't know
comes into my head,
and it is comforting, somehow.
Like a reminder of who I am.

I stand up tall and straight.
'It's all good,
I was just on my way home.'
I meet his eyes exactly.

He grunts,
and the forget-me-not tickles against my palm
as I hold it behind my back,
and head in the direction of the sign
pointing towards the garden gates.

TURNED AROUND

As soon as I exit the park
I realise my mistake:
it's not the same entrance that I walked through
when I came in,
the words *West Gate*
marked in the twirling iron railings.

I stare at my map, confused —
I don't remember which gate I came in from
— *East? North?* —
That gate was next to the bus stop,
and *my* map is planned on the X5 bus.

I can't go back to the park,
and risk another run-in with Wheelbarrow Guy.
I reach for Mum's phone —
what if I should have told her all along,
what if I can't find the park gates,
or figure out how to get home —

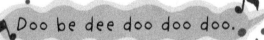

Doo be dee doo doo doo.

Music flows through the air like magic,
a smooth and dancing sound.

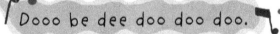

Dooo be dee doo doo doo.

I turn around, trying to see where it is coming from.

Doo be de da da da.

I know that melody.

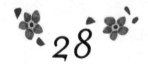

I FOLLOW IT UNTIL I FIND MYSELF

Doo be deeee do bap bap bap.

Its tune is so familiar I know what's coming next,
the beat a whisper as I join its song under my breath:

'Doo be dee dap dap dee.'

And it replies, as if speaking just to me:

Dooo be dee doo doo doo.

Doo be de da da da.

This music, the tune,
flowing down the street from I don't know where —

It's the one Grandma sings more and more
as her memory gets worse.

Dooo be doo bap bap bap.

A tune she knows by heart,
a tune that she must have gotten from —

my dad?

COMPASS

I turn and look around me,
trying to find the direction of the music
coming down the street.
I follow it —
past shops and cafes,
restaurants and boarded-up storefronts,
charity shops like polka dots
spotting along the road.

As I do,
the music gets louder:

A bee dee de dap dap boop bop!

I follow it and follow it until I find myself
on a corner, with two roads to go down.
Which one?
I listen hard,
but I can't tell,
and as I look around I realise it's —

FAMILIAR

The corner I'm standing on.
The corner of not knowing where to go.
On the one side, unfamiliar,
and on the other:

Holy Road.

I pull my backpack off so fast
it swings, hitting me in the chest,
as I grab my notebook,
and pull out the letter from Dad,
and Ray's photo.
There — above where Grandma,
Mum and me are smiling —
the road sign: *Holy Road.*

I hear Ray's voice in my memory:
'*Look — really* look.'

I hold the photo up,
looking at each side
as if it were a puzzle piece.
I line up the edges —
the bushes on the corner,
the sandy colour of the bricks,
the left side leading down
to a street lined with shops,
stone buildings reaching up high —
until it fits exactly,
until I realise I'm standing
in the exact same place,
as in Ray's picture,
the exact same spot
where I held Dad's hand,
ten years ago.

I've done it, I think,
whispering to Grandma in my mind.
I've travelled through time.

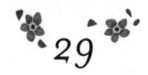

29

ON THE OTHER SIDE OF TIME

DOWN HOLY ROAD

I close my eyes,
and listen to the music around me.
When I open them again
I know which way to go.

I look up at the sign,
Holy Road,
and give it one small nod,
before putting one foot in front of the other,
following the music's lead.

As I walk past storefronts
of tall buildings,
the music gets louder and louder.

The people who pass by
have relaxed looks on their faces,
as if the music has worked its way into their hearts
and calmed them.

I wish it could do the same for me.

My heart is a brass band in my chest,
the boom of a hand against a drum,
DUM-dum-DUM-dum-DUM-dum,
as I follow the sound,
until — here.

The music is coming from here.

THE BEE HIVE

I stop outside a narrow doorway
with a sign, saying:
The Bee Hive Jazz Cafe
and then underneath:
Live Music — Lessons — Jazz.
Formerly Miles's Place.

My thoughts feel like Grandma's cries,
as they shout:
Basim, Basim, Basim!

I did it.
I followed the clues.
I found him.

AFRAID

Laughter jumps out of The Bee Hive,
from a large open window on the first floor
in between the bars of music that pour out,
notes travelling down the street.

I take a shaky breath,
and suddenly feel —
afraid.

Everything I've been working towards
has led me here.

But now that I am here,
now that I'm at the last step,
and all I need to do is knock,
I'm not sure that I can.

I stand there, hand raised,
wanting to knock on The Bee Hive's door,
trying to pluck up the courage,
when I hear footsteps behind it,
and a muffled voice shouting.

The footsteps get nearer,
my heart gets louder,
my body tries to shout:
MOVE!

but it won't.

I hear someone scrambling at the lock behind
the door

it turns

the door opens

my hand is still raised

my face is frozen

and when the door is wide open

and the person steps into the light

and our eyes meet each other's

my whole body is filled with recognition

my whole body is filled with shock

as I say:

'It's you.'

PART 3

A VOICE SO FAMILIAR

'IT'S YOU.'

We both stand,
our eyes mirroring the same expression
of shock
both of us frozen,
his pupils as big
as the round frames of his blue glasses,
his eyebrows so raised
they almost meet his hairline.

I DO THE ONLY THING I CAN THINK TO

I rush forward,
and give him a hug.
'Ray.'

I felt so lost, and even though
I don't know what's going on,
the sight of my friend is like an anchor,
grounding me, safe.

Ray breathes out a big sigh,
hugging me back.
'I knew you'd figure it out.
He said you'd been here before,
when you were a baby,
in his stories about you.'

'He has stories about me?' I say,
leaning back to look at Ray,
hope and panic pulling at me in equal measure.

Ray's face falters for a second,
a question running across it,
as a voice floats down the stairs,
lilting, musical as the jazz which has stopped
its flowing tune.

'I can hear some chatter down there now,'
it calls. 'Everything okay?'

STAIRS

Ray and I look at each other,
and then I am running towards the stairs
and the voice which sounds so familiar,
like someone I've not spoken to in a very long time.

Something in the hazy place
where my one memory of that night lives
stirs, a fragment coming back to me:

that same voice
that same word, 'Okay'.

'It's gonna be okay.'
Strong hands holding me.
'You're going to be okay.'

I take the stairs two by two
and each one takes me closer
to the future
and further into
the past.

WHEN I GET TO THE TOP

I wheel into an open room,
the windows I saw on the street
filling it with light.

Tables, set around in small clusters.
An empty bar in the corner.
A stage, with instruments all over it,
and a tall man in the centre,
alone.

His back is turned to me,
his short afro,
black twisted through with grey,
and there are handprints of fresh soil
on his trousers,
as if he'd just come from —
the garden.

'Dad?' I say.

TIME STOPS

Time seems to slow,
seconds becoming long stretches
like an elastic band stretched double its size
strained to the point of breaking.

The turn of a shoulder first,
his profile older,
then his body facing forward,
his face wide with recognition
and something like heartbreak

as his eyes meet mine

and the elastic band snaps back
with a painful jolt,

as he says to me:

'Nyla?'

ALL I CAN THINK:

It's not him.
It's not my dad.

31

A HEART BREAKS OVER AND OVER

A HEART BREAKS OVER AND OVER

'Who are you?' I manage to say.

The man sets down his saxophone
— *It was him, the music. It came from him* —
he starts to walk towards me gently,
his hands held out,
as if trying to calm a wild thing.

I pull the letter from my pocket.
Dad's letter? The question mark
hammering cracks in the hope I'd had.
As I do, my forget-me-not from the garden
falls to the ground.

'I came here looking for my dad,
I followed this letter,
and a photograph—'
I say, and he reaches to his pocket,
a look of confused shock on his face.

'How did you get that?' he says in disbelief,
looking at the letter clenched tight in my hand.
His eyes follow to the floor,
and he leans down,
picking up the forget-me-not,
cradling it gently.

He looks at it, then back at me.
'Nyla, do you remember me?'

BLUR

That hazy memory blurs again
at the edge of my mind —
that night, the bright lights,
'It's going to be okay.'
The same words I say to myself so often,
with no idea where they came from.

'I—' I open my mouth, to say something,
to ask how he knows my name,
and then remember the music,
the song that I could hear down the street,
the music that led me here.

'That song,' I demand, my whole body shaking —
'what was that song you were playing?'

His face opens and falls
at the same time.

'I wrote it.
It's called "Bee and Ruby".'

B & R.

Not Basim and Ruth.

My knees fall from beneath me,
as if my skeleton has vanished
alongside everything I'd thought was certain
solid clues and facts.

I hear a skittering sound behind me:

'Oomph!'
Ray runs straight into me
then staggers to stand in between us.

'Please,' Ray says, his hands stretched out between us,
'I can explain.'

TWO SIDES TO THIS STORY

'Uncle Bee,' Ray begins,
and my mind sticks on the name,
like the Bee of the song.
'The other night, when I asked you
if you could write a last letter
to the woman you loved long ago,
the one you used to write to always for so long,
the one whose letters you still keep,
even after she vanished —
well,
I knew you would.'

A line from the letter comes back to me like a punch:
Someone asked me: 'What would you do,
if you could write to the love of your past?'

Ray? I think,
at the exact time
his uncle says,
'Raymond?'
His voice filled with the same shock I feel.

Ray's stories from the library,
his impressions, slot into place.

'You wear your heart on your sleeve,
what do you expect?' Ray says,
then remembers himself,
his voice turning serious again:
'I took it.
I saw you write the letter to her,
and I snuck into your room,
and I took it.'

His uncle lowers himself, shaking, into a chair,
his hand resting on the table next to it for support.

'I saw where Nyla lived with her family,'
Ray says, looking between me and his uncle.
'And I thought that if I delivered the letter to Ruby
that maybe it would prompt her to write back to you.'

'Ruby?' My mind races to keep up but Ray,
facing his uncle, doesn't hear me
and continues.

'I didn't tell you I knew where she was,
because you always said the decision had to be hers,
and I didn't know, for sure,
if I was right.
Uncle Bee, in the stories you tell about her,
she was your great love —
and I didn't want to get your hopes up.'

Ray's uncle passes a hand over his face,
as if he could wipe off the shock that rests there,
as Ray turns to me,
his body practically humming with nerves:
'Nyla, I figured out that *you* were related to Ruby
when I saw the birth certificate for your dad.
I mean, I suspected at first —
how many Basim Elachis can there *be*
from Hillworth?'

Ray's eyes are wide behind his glasses,
and my heart pounds within me
following every one of his words.

'I thought Uncle Bee's letter would point you in the right direction,
I thought it would help you *and* Ruby *and* Uncle Bee —
but then, as soon as I left the letter at your house,
I knew I'd done something wrong.'
Ray's face turns solemn,
the corner of his mouth wobbling slightly.
'I knew I'd upset someone,
and just made everything worse.'

My mind goes back to the morning
the letter arrived,
in it hearing the echoes of a cry
from a voice I know and love as well as my own,
the voice of the someone Ray had upset.

Ruby.
Like the song Ray's uncle was playing.
Ruby.
Like the twinkling shine of an old button.
Ruby.
Like the warm of a red wool coat.

Every feeling I've ever felt
crashes within me.

Oh, Grandma.

I meet Ray's eyes.
'Ruby, and—' My jaw wobbles,
and I look to Ray's uncle.
'Bee? The letter was from you,
for my
          grandma?'

Ray nods, stepping closer,
until he is right by my side.

'I didn't know how to tell you,
I just knew it wasn't my story to tell.
And I knew that I had to do something,
to try to help.'

He touches the photograph in my hand.
The one of my family.
The one with the tear down the middle,
a hand reaching from the other side.

'Uncle Bee keeps it in his pocket every day,'
Ray says, his voice so gentle,
so *Ray*. 'I thought if I gave it to you,
that you'd recognise it.
That you'd figure it all out,
and you'd find him,
and all the answers you were looking for.'
He looks at me through glasses misty
with held-back tears.
'I knew you would because you're *you*.
And I thought that, maybe, with all your investigating,
it was something you *needed* to do —
to discover the truth for yourself.'

Ray's words settle around us,
like the small bits of gold that hover
in the soft light streaming in through the wide windows,
illuminating everything.

I watch each one float for a moment.
I feel as if the world has been spun around me,
and I don't know what to hold on to.

Ray's uncle stands up slowly,
and he is tall like a mountain,
his face open, waiting for me to speak.

Now is the time to have all my questions answered.

QUAKE

I thought my voice would be loud,
would be angry and demanding.

But instead, it is the smallest,
whispering quake.

'I thought my dad was alive.'

Saying it out loud
is enough almost for the quake to break,
but I swallow hard,
and keep going:
'And all of this,
the photograph,
the garden,
the letter,
Gra— Ru—'
The words feel so big in my throat,
that I cannot finish them.

'Nyla,' Ray's uncle says softly,
discarded saxophone at his side,
and I turn to him:
the man whose clues I had been following.
The man who was so connected to my family
he'd carried a picture of me in his pocket.
The man who wrote a song I know so well
I can sing its melody.

I meet his eyes and he smiles softly,
as if he understands everything unspoken.
And as if he wants me to go on.

It gives me courage.

And so, my breath shaking in my chest,
I ask: 'What happened?
What happened to my dad?'

32

THE TRUTH

THE TRUTH

'It happened the night Ruby and I
were announcing our engagement.'
Ray's uncle's tone is gentle,
as if knowing how some stories need
to be told with care.
'It was something — something all of us
had wanted for so long.
Your mum was already with us,
and your dad, he rushed home from work,
to celebrate.'
He smiles, and its warmth reaches out
to the weight in my heart,
softens it slightly,
his voice as musical as the song he was playing,
bringing each word together in a melody
all his own.
'Basim was so happy —
he had the kind of smile that could light up a room.'

My eyes flicker to Ray —
to my friend, who also has —
and my heart stutters. Says,
I wish I knew my dad's smile, too.

Watching Bee speak
is like watching someone relive the past,
and his words drag me in with him:
'Nyla, that day, I was there with you.
We'd been reading together,
poetry and nursery rhymes.
Do you remember?'

I shake my head,
grasping at the words within me,
trying to make them come out:
'Mum said he was in a car accident,
but never anything more and then —
after all this — I thought—'
I thought my dad was alive.
I take another shaking breath.
'I need to know the truth.'

Bee nods, and his words
take all hope away
as they grant my request.

'What your mum told you is true.
Your dad was in a car accident
on the way home to be with us.
One of his colleagues was first on the scene,
she did everything she could to try to save him,
but she couldn't.
I'm so sorry, Nyla.
What your mum told you was right:
your dad died.'

GRIEF

It's only when I notice that my face is wet
that I realise I've been crying
through everything he has said.

The truth had been the same all along,
what I'd believed my whole life,
my mum, one of my favourite people in this world
hadn't lied after all,
and yet —

everything feels different, now.

Bee moves forward,
touching my shoulder,
and it runs through me
with a jolt,
like a livewire down into
my memory,
suddenly bringing everything that was blurry
into sharp focus.

A PUZZLE PIECE FITS

I remember now.

That night: the knock at the door,
flashing lights against the curtains,
illuminating Grandma and Mum's faces,
red and blue, shocked and distraught.

Mum moving in slow motion to answer it,

Grandma making a sound I'd never heard before.

And the hands.
The hands holding me,
and the words:
'It's going to be okay.'
The words I'd learned to repeat to myself,
whenever I felt worried or afraid.

I look up at Bee's face,
and it's like everything suddenly slots
into the time it's supposed to be in:
his hand, the very same one
so warm in my memory,
pulling me out of the past
into the present.

And I —
run.

I run as fast
and as hard
as I can.

33

MAPLESS

RUN

I run,
so fast,
away from Ray's shout
and Bee's outstretched palm,
the photograph and letter still clutched in my hands,
the stairs of The Bee Hive
shaking under me.

I race past the shops
and houses I walked past earlier,
Holy Road a distant blur.

I run past takeaways and restaurants and houses and parks.
Past traffic lights and road junctions and building sites.
Past primary schools and churches and tower blocks,
over pavement and grass and tarmac.

I run until I am out of myself and my life,
wanting to leave every question and every hope behind.

MAPLESS

That's the thing about running.
Sometimes it's about getting to where you are going quickly,
and sometimes it's about just getting away —
about everything moving you so far far far beyond
what you can no longer bear to stand in.

It's like everything I've learned
from Ray and his uncle
has thrown my compass away.
I run like a star exploding.

When I finally stop,
I am breathless.
I am great gasps of air.
I am palms of hands flat on thighs.
Back bent. Heaving lungs.
Sweat clammy in my hair.
I lean back against a brick wall,
grateful that no one can see me,
as with each pant of breath,
the truth comes crashing into me,
no matter how hard
I try to fight it.

AT THE END OF THE DAY

I wanted my dad to be alive.

More than I've ever wanted
anything before.

So much
that just by wanting it
I hoped it could be true.
It had to exist
because of how much I needed it to.
I realise I didn't care about the reason he'd stayed away,
or why he couldn't tell us.

I'd just wanted him here.

And now he's not even a letter.
He's nowhere.
And I'm back.

Half Orphan.
Half Untold Story.
Missing.

I DON'T KNOW WHERE I AM

When I'm able to open my eyes,
my breath steady and slow,
it's like squinting into light for the first time.

Everything seems bigger, somehow.
The world around me feeling
slightly strange,
my insides scrubbed raw.

I feel like the most fragile thing.

Something in my pocket buzzes,
and I pull out Mum's phone,
see her office number.
She's trying to find it.

I let it ring,
and when it stops,
I see the time:
3.30 p.m.

Grandma.

I GOT LOST IN TIME

I got lost in time, too:
and I returned to the present,
way too late.

I look up, take everything around me in.
I have to be there for Grandma.

But I've no idea
where I am.

The image in my mind,
of Grandma alone,
abandoned outside our house,
is heavier than anything else,
than any sinking feeling
or loss of hope of finding my dad,
of anything I have ever felt.

She counts on me.
I can't let her down.

I look around me — didn't I run
past a rush of green trees,
past Greenwood Park
already?

The streets look sort of familiar,
like the ones I saw when I was on the bus.

I pull out Mum's phone,
relieved that the battery is still above 50 per cent,
pull up the map app,
and type in my address,
hoping to find a bus home.
But next to the little bus logo
is a single struck-through line
/
No buses from here.

And then on the screen,
the image of a person walking,
and the time it takes: 40 minutes.

I stare at the phone in disbelief.
Somehow, I must have run so far,
that I ran halfway back home,
without knowing where I was,
or where I was going.

I can make it.

If I run,
I can make it back on time.

MY LEGS TEACH ME A LESSON

As I start to jog,
blue dot bobbing in my hand showing me the way,
I think about how this time
I am running towards something,
someone,
not running away,
and how they feel different in my heart,
but the same in my legs.

When I left Ray's uncle's,
my mind left my body too,
but my legs, somehow, they knew,
where to take me,
to get me closer to home.

As the streets start to take shape,
into something I recognise,
I think about how you can be
in totally unfamiliar territory,
yet only around the corner from home,
if you let yourself be your own compass.

When I am ten minutes away,
I shut down the map on Mum's phone.

I know where I am.
I can take it from here.

I can be my own guide.

34

THE FIRST THREAD OF MY STORY

WHEN I GET TO MY STREET

I can see her in the distance:
sat on the wall by my pebbledash house.

How could Maria just leave her there?
Grandma could wander off with anybody.

I was meant to be there for Grandma,
it's the one responsibility I have,
to look after the people in my present,
instead of chasing a foolish past.

My legs pick up their pace,
beyond what I thought they could do.

They are strong; stronger.

I run fast; faster.

I can bridge the distance between her and me.

YOU SEE THE FULL PICTURE
WHEN YOU GET UP CLOSE

Grandma is all I see,
and as I get close she looks up at me.
'Sweetie!'

Warmth spreads through me,
as I throw my body at her,
and wrap her in a hug.
She squeezes me back tight.

At my door behind me,
I hear a crunch on the gravel,
and a hesitant, familiar, voice:

'Hello, Nyla,' Miss Haldi says.

A LIBRARIAN CALLS

Miss Haldi holds up a stack of books,
as if in explanation.
'I came to drop these off ...'
Her words trail.

Grandma taps my arm,
gesturing at Miss Haldi.
'Pretty guest,'
Grandma says,
as she marches
towards the front door,
and waits expectantly
for me to open it.

SWEETIE TEA

It feels strange,
having Miss Haldi inside my house.
I worry what she will think of it.

Miss Haldi moves like a natural —
as if she knows instinctively where Grandma's chair is,
putting on the TV low in the background,
and laying her fidget blanket down.

I go to the kitchen to make tea for them both
— *Do I offer Miss Haldi biscuits? Do we even have any?* —
Grandma starts chatting,
and Miss Haldi chats back.

'She thinks I'm a nurse,'
Miss Haldi says to me in a low voice, as I pass her tea over,
and hold Grandma's lukewarm one to her lips
(I never make it too hot in case it spills).

'You're a beautiful nurse, too,'
Grandma says to me.

'Grandma, I'm Sweetie,' I reply.
'I'm your granddaughter.'

Grandma smiles at me like I'm a miracle,
and she replies,
'My beautiful nurse related to me.
My beautiful Sweetie.'
And I laugh, unsure if Grandma is confused,
or if she is actually seeing me,
recognising all that I am
and all that I do.

Either way,
regardless of how Grandma's time moves,
she sees me.

And wrapped in her ruby-red coat,
I see her, too.

AS GRANDMA DOZES, MISS HALDI EXPLAINS

'When I got here,
I was ringing the bell
and then a bus from the care home arrived
and, well — I sensed it might cause
problems if you weren't home —
and when they asked if I was the new home carer I just—'
Miss Haldi's hands fall at her side,
with a shrug.

She had covered for me.
She has my back.
I sigh out with relief.
'Thank you,' I say.

'Nyla,' Miss Haldi says, gently,
and when she asks me this time,
as she always does,
if everything is okay,
I do the one thing I've wanted everyone else to do,
but struggled to do myself:
tell the truth.

MISS HALDI GETS HER ANSWER

'It began,' I say,
and I don't know
where to start.

'Miss Haldi,' I say,
and her name is like a fixed point
that brings her eyes
 — open, patient —
directly into mine.

I reach into the sea of emotion,
surging within me.
It is there that I find the first thread
of my story.

'I wanted to know who I am,'
I say, and the sea pours out.
'I wanted to find my dad.'

I TELL MISS HALDI EVERYTHING

From trying to find my dad,
to figuring out if something is racist,
to looking after Grandma,
and all my investigating —
everything that led me to The Bee Hive today.

And then it starts building in my chest.
Now the secret's out in the world,
and Miss Haldi knows the truth,
my feelings want to join them,
and I take One
                    Big
                        Shaking
                                Scary
                            Strong
                        Breath
and release,
as all the tears
come pouring out.

WHEN I STOP, MISS HALDI SAYS:

'Nyla,'
and her voice cuts through
everything else.
'You've been so very brave.'

MISS HALDI MAKES A VERY GOOD POINT

'You're being so hard on yourself,'
she says. 'You've gone on such a huge journey,
and though I know it didn't end where you wanted it to,
perhaps
where you have found yourself
still has what you were looking for,
just not in the way you expected.'

I nod, running my sleeve
along my nose,
to wipe away the snot.
'I did find something,' I say.
'Or someone — but not the person
I wanted most.'

Miss Haldi sets down her tea.
'I am so very sorry, Nyla,
about your dad.'

And though her words are so simple,
and I've heard them said to Mum a thousand times,
something about having Miss Haldi say them to me,
her seeing my grief,
calms the cries inside me.

'Thank you,' I whisper.

'What do you want to do?'
Miss Haldi asks.
Her emphasis on the *you*
makes me pause.

It's a question I've been asking myself for so long,
but it feels different, having someone else ask it.

'I think I have to tell Mum.'
I say, and Miss Haldi nods,
listening. 'And — I think you're right,
about how even though I didn't find my dad—'
I gulp, tears threatening again.
'I have to go back to the person I did find.
And uncover the rest of the story.'

Miss Haldi smiles gently.
'I think that's wise,' she says.

THE LIBRARIAN'S WISDOM

We finish our tea as we talk through my decision.
Miss Haldi sets her cup down,
and instead picks up the books
she brought with her,
as if holding them helps her figure out
what to say.

'Yesterday, outside the library,'
she begins, 'I saw that boy,
the one who I think
had something to do with our fire alarm.
The one who should never
have treated you like that.
I reckon he saw me, too,
because he ran away,
though he didn't bet on me chasing him —
I gave him the biggest talking-to of his life!'

I laugh at the thought of Miss Haldi,
holding a library book above her head,
chasing Harry down.

'I'm pretty sure the look on your face alone
got the message across,' I say,
as I see a flicker of it cross her features.

Miss Haldi smiles softly.
'It did. But my words did, too.
I'm going to talk to the school about the fire alarm,
and — if it's okay with you —
I can mention what I witnessed, too.
This isn't something that should be ignored.'

I can't help but think back to Uncle Bee's words,
and how Miss Haldi might be one of the people
who help water my story,
and who let me sit
in the shade of theirs.
'Thank you,' I say.

'I was so worried for you, Nyla,
though I can see that you know
how to handle yourself.
I didn't know what I could do to help—'

'You do help, Miss Haldi,'
I say, and she looks down,
as if hiding the wobble in her throat.

MISS HALDI SPEAKS THE TRUTH:

'I wish I could tell you it was always going to be easy.
I wish I could say you'll never face another Harry again,
and that people will always see the truth,
and not the lies,
or that injustice will go away,
and that you won't have times in your life
when you'll feel exactly this way,
or cry from this same place —
that same spot in you that misses your dad,
or has been called words I refuse to say.
But you might, Nyla. You might.
And so, instead, what I can tell you is that you are brave:
and that there are things about you that are so special,
and so strong, and that all of the questions
this world has given you —
you can answer them.
You can decide them for yourself.
You can choose home in yourself,
for yourself.
You are not bad.
You are not wrong.
You are living through a world
that has inherited so many difficulties,
and yet you are thriving.
And there are others in this world
who are fighting those difficulties,
doing good things, making a difference,
making hope.
Who took all those questions,
and took all their brave,
and chose to create change.
Just like your friend Ray did,
when he tried to help.
And just like you did,
when you went searching for your dad
today.'

MISS HALDI'S GIFT

Miss Haldi slides the books toward me:
one brown,
one pink,
one yellow and purple.

'No matter what happens in your story,'
— her voice is soft, but clear —
'you have the power to choose how to tell it,
rather than letting it tell you.'

I reach out, and give Miss Haldi a hug.

Behind us, Grandma rouses.
'Sweetie, help me up!'
she demands,
and I do.

'Are you okay, Grandma?'
I ask.

'Of course!' she says.
'I just wanted a hug too!'
And with that she squeezes us both.

'Thank you for everything,' I say
when we let go.

Miss Haldi nods,
in that gentle way of hers.

'Of course. It's what librarians are for.'

ANSWER

Our doorbell rings
trilling through the house.

'Someone's coming for tea!'
Grandma exclaims.

I creep to the door,
Miss Haldi hovering behind me.

What if it's Ray's uncle?
I think with sudden panic.
What if it's Ray?

But another voice,
the one Miss Haldi encouraged me to find,
tells me:

You can do this, Nyla.

35

A SECRET HIDDEN IN A LITTLE RED COAT

I OPEN MY FRONT DOOR

The first thing I see is sequins:
a sparkling pink dress,
floor-length,
like something out of a movie set.

I look up, and when I see the dress's owner,
I expect to hear an angry shout
along the lines of:
'NYLA ELACHI,
YOU'VE LET ME DOWN.'

But instead,
Jess jumps towards me,
wrapping her arms around me
without a word.

MY TURN TO APOLOGISE

'I'm so sorry,'
I whisper, into Jess's hair,
the sequins of her dress
prickling my chin.
'It's just today was the only day I could—'

'I know,' Jess says, before I finish.
'When you didn't show up for school this morning,
I looked at the email attachment and figured it out.
You're not the only detective here.'

I laugh,
and hug her even tighter.

'Are you okay?' she whispers.
'Did you find your dad?'

I shake my head against her shoulder.
'No. But I found a story
that I think has been waiting to be told
for a long, long time.'

A ROUND OF APPLAUSE

I promise Jess I'll tell her everything,
I just need some time.
I think about Ray's insistence
that it wasn't his *story to tell*.
I have to do this — tell this — right.

As we stand in my hallway,
I look Jess up and down.
'Why are you dressed like this?'

Her pink sequins glitter in the light.
'I came straight from the rehearsal,' she says,
as if it's obvious.

'You walked here in your costume?'

Jess wiggles her eyebrows at me.
'*Mais oui, mon amie!*
I figured it was about time
we gave the folks of this town
their own bit of celebrity glamour.'

She twirls,
and as she does,
I hear the sound of clapping,
and turn to see Grandma watching us,
her eyes filled with delight,
at the sparkle of Jess's dress.

'Beautiful!' Grandma says,
and Miss Haldi claps too.

Jess walks towards Grandma:
'Thank you, Grandma Farida.'
She loops her arm through hers.
'It's been so long since I last saw you,

chérie, now tell me — I hear you've been doing
a spot of time-travel,
is that right?'

WHAT TO DO NEXT

Jess walks through to the living room,
still linking arms with Grandma,
introducing herself to Miss Haldi
with a swept bow and a:
'Jess, local celebrity.'

I take my chance,
and sneak upstairs
with Mum's phone.
I make two calls.
And hope that with them,
I can make things right.

TWO HALVES MAKE A WHOLE

When I come back downstairs,
Miss Haldi and Jess chatting in the kitchen,
I go to Grandma, sat in her chair.

'Grandma,' I say,
'I have something to show you –
something you might recognise.'

Grandma frowns.
'Are you okay, Sweetie?
You look so sad.'

I shake my head.
'I'm okay. Everything, I think,
is going to be okay.'

I reach into my pocket,
and pull out the photograph Ray gave me.
The one of Grandma, Mum and me,
and the hand that is reaching –
the hand that has always been reaching.

Grandma looks at it for a long time,
and when at last she looks at me,
I can see the tears in her eyes.

She stands up slowly
and, taking my arm,
leads me to the hallway
where her small red coat
hangs by the door,
waiting for her to put it on.
Waiting for her to go.
She opens its inside pocket, gently,
and pulls out the slip of a photograph,
a torn edge of white running down its middle.

She has always carried this with her,
I realise.
Always kept it in her red coat,
close enough to her heart
to feel its beat.

She places it together with the one in my hands.
The truth was there
all along.

THE TIME IS NOW

THE TIME IS NOW

When Mum comes home,
the house is quiet.

Miss Haldi and Jess left half an hour ago,
after a conversation that included
Jess inviting Miss Haldi to the school play,
and Miss Haldi saying how much she loves
the dramatic arts,
and promising she'll come.

I hugged them both again
before they left,
and hoped that my touch could show
how much they mean to me.

When Mum walks through the door,
her face pale,
her lips thin,
I hope I can do the same,
that I can start this conversation,
the secrets we've been keeping from each other,
with us in the same place.

'Mum,' I say,
as I wrap my arms around her.
'I've got so much to tell you.'

HERE

Mum runs her hands down my hair.
'I'm here,' she says.

And I realise that, perhaps, after all,
that was one of the things
I truly wanted
as part of my search.
I just didn't know.

When I phoned Mum,
and asked her to come home
as soon as she could,
her first question was worry:
'Did something happen?
Are you feeling worse?
Is Grandma okay?'

I could hear the rush in her chest
like the one I get in mine:
the struggle to keep things under control,
the hope they won't get any worse.

'I found Bee,' I whispered,
and I heard a sharp inhale of breath
on the other end of the line.

I look at her now,
both of us sat across from each other in the kitchen,
Grandma snoring away in the background,
clutching her photograph taped back together,
finally complete.

Mum's eyes are red.
I wonder how I could ever think
that she didn't care,
or that she was hiding things from me
for any reason
other than trying her best.

Because she's like me,
I think.

And it's that thought
that finally makes me reach out my hand,
and speak.

EVERYTHING, AGAIN

Mum listens.
Occasionally she looks angry, upset, confused,
but she doesn't interrupt me.

When I tell her about not finding Dad's death certificate,
and about overhearing her phone call,
thinking that he could be alive,
she looks so sad
that I imagine I'm seeing all the weights on me
multiplied.

When I tell her about Sister Amina,
she shakes her head:
'It's not what you think.'

She asks to meet Miss Haldi,
and when I tell her about The Bee Hive,
her jaw wobbles,
and a small tear runs down her face.

'I'm sorry,' I whisper.

Mum shakes her head.
'I wish you'd spoken to me,
and not carried all of this alone.
I'm sorry, too.'

Mum rests her face in her hands for a second,
and sighs. It's like
the weight of our world
is carried there in our breath,
hanging around us on the table
ready for both of us to pick it up
and hold it together.

'The certificate,' she says, looking up.
'I keep it separate,
because I can't bear to look at it.
And the phone call you overheard.
It — it wasn't about your dad ...
at least, not directly,' she says.
'It was about Grandma.'

ALL ROADS LEAD BACK TO GRANDMA

'Is she okay?!' is my first question,
my mind panicked.

Mum reaches her hand across the table,
and then her whole body
pulls me close.

I've missed you, I think.

'Your grandma's fine — well,
except for her time-travelling,
but the doctors say she's doing okay —
and a huge part of that is down to
how happy she is getting to see you.'

I nod, warm against Mum's chest.

'But as time goes on — and she's okay for now,
Nyla, she really is — as time goes on,
she's going to need more and more care,
and it's not something that you
or I
can do.
And care—'

And I know the words
before she has even spoken them.
'—costs money?' I say.

'Yes.'

'And we don't have any,' I say
like a statement,
feeling the weight of that full stop.

Mum pauses,
hesitates, then says:

'Well, that's the thing. When I said,
on the phone, that your dad left —
I was talking about what he left.
I was talking about money.'

DAD'S SURPRISE

'It's not much: a small pot of savings
your dad used to call his Adventure Fund.
He wanted to save something
for living — that's what he always used to say.
And so, he'd put a small amount
to one side for a house, or a holiday, or you.
He had so many plans.'

Mum's voice cracks.
All this time, I've been focused
on how I feel about my dad —
I've forgotten what it must be like
for her.

'It's not much, Nyla — it's less
than some might spend on fancy food in a year —
but it was his. And he wanted it to go to you.
So, I kept it, like a promise.'

My brilliant, brave mum.

'And now we need it for Grandma?' I ask.

Mum sighs.

'I've been trying to save as much as I can,
for when the time comes.
The cost of keeping Grandma with us,
of having someone help care for her at home —
it's so much, Nyla.
Even with your dad's money,
it's not enough to stretch even past a few months.
Maria — that's who I was on the phone to —
we've been trying to apply for funding to cover it,
so that I can keep the promise I made to your dad,
to save this money for you,

and keep the promise I made to Grandma,
to look after her in her own home.
But it gets harder and harder as time goes on,
there's pressure on every penny.'

'I don't need the money,' I say in a rush.
'I didn't know about it before,
it doesn't make a difference—'

Mum shakes her head.
'Whichever way I look at it,
I feel like I can't escape breaking my promise to
myself, and to you:
to give you a childhood without
the weight of the world on your shoulders.
To give you what me, your dad,
and Grandma
never had.
And more than all that'
— and here Mum's face turns fierce —
'it's not right, Nyla.
To be so squeezed,
and so short,
just trying to take care of the people you love.
And your dad's money,
his Adventure Fund,
it's a dream I wanted to protect too —
a gift, even though he's not here,
I wanted it to be a gift he could give to you.'

I hold Mum tight.

'You've given me the best of all, Mum,'
I say. 'You've given me Grandma,
and you've given me
you.'

HUG

As I hug Mum,
I find myself repeating the words,
that were once repeated to me:
'It's gonna be okay.'

'It is,' she says. 'Especially when
my genius here is so good
at finding the things I can't.'

I look at her quizzically.
'What do you mean?

'Bee, Nyla. You found him.
Your grandma and him, they had some agreement,
to take time away from each other after your dad died.
She blamed herself, I think.
She told me they wrote letters,
and that one day she'd write to him to come back.
Then, as her time-travelling got worse,
it cut her off from him.
She forgot to send her letters, forgot his address too.
He never wrote a return one on his envelopes.'

Mum looks away,
memories of her own investigating
playing across her face.
'I've been searching,
trying to find him.
I didn't know he'd bought the jazz club —
we used to go there when you were young,
and I didn't even think — it's been so long.
I didn't even know he was in Hillworth,
as he'd moved from his old address.
And you found him for me, for Grandma, Nyla.
You did that.'

And then Mum says the words
that I'd hoped so much to hear:

'I'm so proud of you.'

GOODNIGHT, GRANDMA

Later, Mum and I kiss Grandma goodnight.
'You've got a big day tomorrow,' I say.
'You're going to see someone you've not seen
in a very long time.'

'A visitor, Sweetie?'
Grandma asks back. 'Who?'

I sing the first tune of the beat
I know now by heart,
hoping its sound will reach her
no matter where she is in time:

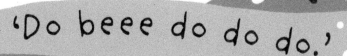

'Do beee do do do.'

Grandma smiles,
and closes her eyes.

Mum and I creep out of her room,
the photograph propped on Grandma's bedside table.

As we close the door, I hear Grandma hum
the next part of the melody:

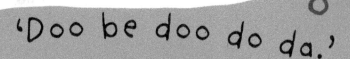

'Doo be doo do da.'

MUM MAKES ONE LAST PROMISE

Mum tucks me in,
the duvet snug against my neck,
my feet cosy and warm.
She sits on the edge of my bed.

'I'm sorry I've let my sadness
stand in the way of telling you
about all the wonderful parts of your dad,'
she says.
I reach out of my cocoon
to hold her hand.
'I never imagined the impact it would have on you —
how it would send you on this search.
I know you must miss him, too.'

I meet her eyes in the dark.
'I do. But I understand.
I know you were just trying your best.'

Mum's hand is soft against my cheek.
'Will you let me make you one last promise,
Sweet Pea?'

I nod. 'Of course, Mum.'

And she kisses my head softly,
as I slowly fall asleep.

'I promise to tell you stories.
So many stories,
all about your dad.'

VISITORS COMING FOR TEA

SATURDAY MORNING

After we tidy the whole house,
Mum picks out Grandma's best outfit
and I do her hair,
her curls free from their braid,
framing her face.

I hold up the mirror,
and show her.

'Beautiful!' she says,
for once seeing in herself
what she sees in everyone else.
I kiss her cheek.

'You're a treasure, Grandma,'
I say.

She looks at me,
her brown eyes big, and wide.

'You know, Sweetie,'
she says. 'I was once
somebody's Ruby.
I was once
a treasured jewel.'

I kiss both of her cheeks.
'You still are,'
I say, and smile.

THE DRAWER

Grandma's hand wobbles
over her dressing table drawer,
as she opens it gently.

Inside are old lipsticks,
strings of costume jewellery,
and stray buttons
from her box.

She reaches a hand in,
and then pulls out
a stash of paper.

Letters. All bound together.

She looks at me, her face serious.
'There's someone waiting for me, Sweetie,'
she says. 'Only, I don't know how to write back,
to tell them where I am.'

Before I can answer, I hear a knock
on Grandma's bedroom door.

Mum smiles as she says:
'It's time.'

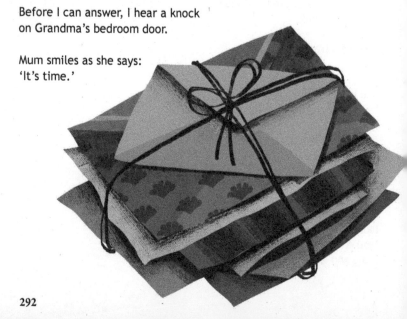

VISITORS FOR TEA

The sun is bright
as we lead Grandma out to the garden.

The visitors I invited over the phone yesterday
are due to arrive any minute.

In the garden, Jess sits at Grandma's side.
She insisted on being here,
joking that it's because
she didn't want to miss the drama,
but really,
I know it's because she cares.

When the doorbell rings,
I see Mum jump,
then smooth her jeans,
like trying to smooth her nerves.

We answer it together.

REUNION

When Mum sees Bee,
she makes a noise
like a gasp
meeting a cry.

'Bertie Edwards, as I live and breathe,' she says,
and then they are hugging,
and they are laughing,
and she is saying, 'It's so good to see you,'
and he is saying, 'My gosh,
you look so well,
and Nyla, you must be
so proud.'

'Bertie?' I say,
when Bee comes towards me,
and he laughs:
'Bertie, Bee, Uncle,' he says.
'I have many names.'

Me too, I think. *Like Sweet Pea,
and Sweetie.*

I've been called many names
— including ones that hurt —
but I know that the names we are given
from the people who love us
hold some of that love inside them.
And how the most powerful names
can be the ones we choose
for ourselves.

I decide to try and show Bertie — Ray's uncle — Bee,
how much he means
to me.
'Can I call you Uncle Bee?'

And then my feet are off the floor,
as Uncle Bee sweeps me up in a big hug,
and spins me round.

When he puts me back down,
a small face peers at me from the door.

'I think that's a yes,' Ray says.

A BETTER PLACE

It's quiet as we look at each other,
each one not knowing where to start.

I decide to begin with what matters most:

'Thank you, Ray,' I say,
and he looks up,
eyes round and open.

'You understand?' he asks.

This has always been an important question
between my friend and me.

I nod. 'I do. Without you ...
none of this would have happened.'

'Without you, too,' he says.

I grin. 'We did it together;
we brought them back to each other.'

Ray grins back. 'We did, didn't we?'

'Ray, you know how you said,
ages ago in the library,
that you wanted to make the world
a better place?'

Ray nods.

'Well, you have,' I say.
'You definitely, definitely have.'

'Thank you,' Ray says.

'What for?' I ask.

'For knowing I was helping.
For seeing who I am.'

I throw my arm over his shoulder,
as we step into my house.

'Thank you, Ray, for seeing me, too.'

38

B&R

BEE AND RUBY

Uncle Bee sits on the sofa,
where Miss Haldi sat what feels like months ago
but was only yesterday.
Time can be funny, that way.
You can't control it —
how fast it moves,
or how slow.

I set Uncle Bee's mug of tea down,
and he begins to tell his story.

'Your grandma and I were sweethearts,'
he says, and we listen:
me and Mum and Ray.

'We met after we both first arrived in the UK.
We'd spend every minute together.
She loved to dance, and I loved jazz,
and her.
We'd go to Miles's Place
— that's what The Bee Hive was called,
before I bought it a few years back —
and on our walks home,
we'd sit by the bandstand in Greenwood Park,
and plan our future together.
That's where she gave me my name: Bee.
Because she said I was always wanting

to make honey music,
but the way I practised
sounded like a lot of buzzing.'

We both laugh, picturing Grandma's cheeky way.
It sounds just like her.

'I called her my Ruby,' he says, softly.
'The jewel of my eye. I'd tell her,
"You're my treasure,"
and she was.'

It's like the voice from his letter
has come alive.

'We wanted to get married,
but her family didn't approve.
They wanted her to be with
someone from the same country as them,
someone of the same faith,
with a fancy job they could understand,
not a jazz musician with no money to his name.'

My brow furrows.
'Why weren't they just happy for you?'

Uncle Bee inhales deeply.
'I think that the racism
your great-grandparents grew up with ...
it chewed them up, and spat them out,
and twisted how they felt about themselves,
and everyone else. Including me.
It was an ugly, ugly thing.
Your great-grandparents told your grandma
if she didn't marry someone
they selected for her, that they would never be happy.
She fought them, but then her father took ill —
and the family said it was because of the stress.

He begged her on his sick bed to do what they asked.
So, she did.'

My chest feels hollow, at what Uncle Bee
and Grandma suffered.
'I'm so sorry,' I say.

Uncle Bee smiles softly,
as if half of him is caught in the memory of the story,
and half here with us.
'They may have tried to separate us,
but, Nyla — you and Ray,
you brought us back.'

I nod, but as
I think of my great-grandparents' legacy,
it doesn't feel like enough.

'I want the future to be better,' I say.
'Even if I don't know what to do about,
or how to understand,
the past.'

Uncle Bee takes my hand.
'We do it by looking after each other,'
he whispers.
'And by remembering,
and honouring,
and listening to each other's stories.'

I look up at him, meeting his eye,
as if his story lives there,
emotion radiating from the vibrant brown of his iris,
as much as it does from his words.

'I'd like to keep listening to yours,' I whisper,
with a smile.

'Well, good job, because I've got many a tale.'
Uncle Bee winks, with a warm glance at Ray,
who smiles too, as if he knows this well.

'How did you find your way back to each other?' I ask.
'At the club, you said were going to get engaged,
on the night my dad ... died?'

I hesitate on the last word.
I have to get used to saying it again.
Uncle Bee meets my eye,
and pauses for a moment,
as if giving me space.

'That *fool* her parents made her marry' —
I meet Ray's eye, the corner of both our mouths twitching,
at the familiar Grandma and Bee word —
'he left while your grandma was pregnant with your dad.
After that, she wanted to decide her future for herself.
That's why you, your dad,
have the name "Elachi":
She came up with it
and gave it to you all.
She wanted to start afresh.'

I've never felt prouder to have my name,
now I know the story in it:
one of struggle,
but also
one of strength.
One of going your own way.

GRANDMA TRIES TO KEEP EVERYONE SAFE

'But, Uncle Bee, why didn't you get married
straight away?'

He throws up his hands.

'We couldn't get a hold of the fool for a divorce,
that's why we waited so long —
it was only when we heard that he'd passed away
that we could marry officially.
It didn't change the fact that we were a family, though:
me, your grandma, your dad. Then your mum.
And you.'

'But, if everything was good,' I ask,
confused, 'why did everything fall apart
after Dad?'

Uncle Bee shifts in his seat,
his face falling serious.
'When your dad died,
your grandma, well, she felt like her happiness
had caused it.'
The 'h' in 'her' and 'happiness'
disappears as Uncle Bee speaks,
and I imagine for a moment,
letter after letter disappearing
in Grandma's mind back then,
h
   a
      p
         p
       i
    n
   e
      s
        s

falling,
floating away.

'Basim had been rushing to celebrate with us,
and in her mind, if he hadn't been —
he might have still been alive.
She thought if we were apart from each other,
if she punished herself and denied that happiness,
that it would somehow keep us all safe:
me, you, your mum. Like her being happy
had caused one of the things she loved the most
to be taken away,
and she didn't want anyone else to get hurt.'

I look at Grandma's chair,
wishing I could hug her.
'That's why you wrote letters instead?'

Uncle Bee nods. 'All the time.
That's how we got each other through
the grief. We always intended
to reunite — but then her letters
got less and less frequent.
And when I couldn't find her,
I thought it was because she didn't want to be found,
and though I didn't understand —
I had to respect that.
I didn't know that it was because—'
His voice trembles.

'—because she'd started her time-travelling?'
I whisper.

'Yes,' Uncle Bee says.
'And then you showed up yesterday.
And everything changed.'

THE TIME-TRAVELLERS
RETURN FROM THE PAST

I hug Uncle Bee so close,
so fiercely, that the tears on both of our cheeks
mingle: as if his story is overflowing out of both of us,
until I can't tell which is mine
and which is his.

'Thank you for being my family,
when I didn't even know,' I say.

He squeezes me back,
and I feel like we're mirroring the past in reverse:
me holding him in the same way he did me
on that night that changed all of our lives.

I pick up Uncle Bee's hand —
the one that played jazz,
the one that Grandma loved
and lost and loved again,
the one that was let down, let go,
the one that suffered others' racism,
the one that was strong when I was small.
I pick up all of the past that lives within his five fingers,
and all of the future still to come, and lead him
out into the garden.

To Ruby,
waiting there.

IT'S TIME

Uncle Bee's legs shake, slightly,
as we head out of the back door.
'Not as young as I used to be!' he jokes,
but he'd been a young man in my head,
as I listened to his story.

For a moment, I feel sad
that my dad will never get to be
that way — to have achy legs,
or wrinkles formed by laughter.

It's not something I can change,
I know that now.
But it is something
I can find a way
to live with.

I take Uncle Bee by one arm,
Ray taking the other,
as Mum goes ahead,
to prepare Jess and Grandma.

I see Mum first, the way she turns,
and then ushers Jess away slightly to the side
(my friend trying not to gawk,
Mum trying not to cry).

I let go of Uncle Bee's arm gently.

Some steps,
I know,
you have to take on your own.

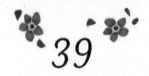

39

THE BEST DAY

TRUTH

If I could capture time,
if I could store it in a box
or in myself,
then this moment
would be one I would want to always remember.

The light is soft
as Uncle Bee walks up our garden,
towards where Grandma sits on a white plastic chair.
I don't know if it's
the tears brimming in my eyes
or the sun
but the grass seems greener,
and something about it reminds me
of Greenwood Park,
as if two places had layered over each other.

Uncle Bee walks towards Grandma,
and she looks up.

'Oh,' she says.

She reaches out a wavering hand
then pushes herself up.

'Oh.'

A wavering leg.
A wavering step.

'Oh.'

A wavering gasp.

And suddenly they are both hugging.

Suddenly they are both in their own time.

'My Bee,' I hear her gasp from a distance.
'You came back.'

And I see his shoulders shake.

'Always, Ruby,' he says.

SPACE

We watch them talk from a distance,
and Mum's hand rests gently on my shoulder.
I wonder if she can see what I see:

the way Uncle Bee holds Grandma's hand,
hers curved into his, like the curve of a *B*
blended with an *R*.

The way Grandma is slightly returned to us —
not perfect, perhaps not in the same time as us,
but more *her*. More *here* than she was before.

I don't know if she thinks
she is talking to Uncle Bee
as two older people in their seventies.
Or if she is talking to him as the young people
they were when they first met,
or as a woman, passionate, in her twenties,
fighting for what was right;
or as a mother,
filled with heartbreak;
or as herself from every stage of her whole life,
of the life they should have had together.
And while I can't change the past,
I am glad that all my time-travelling
led to this: to Grandma talking as her,
as all of these things,
and to Bee talking back.

And something in her smile as she looks at him
spells out that same word
I read at the end of Uncle Bee's letter:

'Always.'

BASIM AND ME

After a while,
Uncle Bee gestures
towards where we all sit.

'Ruby,' he says.
'There's someone I'd like you to meet.
He's heard a lot about you,
and he played a brave part,
in bringing us together today.'

Grandma nods,
and I silently say to Ray
with my smile:
Thank you.
He smiles back,
and we walk towards them together.

When Grandma sees Ray,
        his sprained arm,
                    and round blue glasses
                            taking over his face,
                she shouts:

'Basim!
Basim,
you came back!'

UNCLE BEE EXPLAINS

Uncle Bee laughs
a little at first,
then a lot,
his whole body moving.

'I knew them glasses reminded me
of someone,'
he says, wiping a tear of laughter from his eye,
as Grandma grabs Ray,
and presses his face to her chest,
refusing to let go.

Ray looks at me,
panicked for a second,
then seems to accept his fate,
patting her arms gently,
as she holds him close.

'When your dad,' Uncle Bee says,
'was your and Raymond's age,
he used to wear glasses exactly like this.
He said they made him feel cool.'

'You ran away! You came back!'
Grandma scolds Ray in the background.

Uncle Bee picks it up,
translates.
'One night, oh, we had such a big fight —
though I can't even remember what about now,
but, oh, it was a real howler.' Uncle Bee laughs,
before continuing the story.
'And he ran away, and in doing so tried to hide
in a tree house — he was always an adventurous type —
"to prove he could do it all on his own" he said.
He fell, and broke his arm,

and had a cast not unlike this—'
Uncle Bee gestures to Ray,
who is trapped in Grandma's embrace,
before casually going on.
'In fact, I think that's when he first decided
he wanted to be a nurse.
But he was so embarrassed
to tell anyone he'd hurt himself,
that he didn't come home.'

Mum nudges me, whispers:
'Adventurous? Independent? Sound familiar?'

I laugh, leaning in to her.

Uncle Bee continues:
'Three days that boy stayed away.
Your grandma worried herself
up to the high heavens
and back.'

'It all makes sense ...' I say.
'... when Ray dropped the letter at the door.'

Ray murmurs a yes in the background,
from between Grandma's arms.

'And at the supermarket?'
I ask.

To which Ray replies:
'The big one near Hillworth?'

'Yes — that was you too?'

'Yes — though I couldn't hear what she was saying.
All I knew was that an old woman was chasing me —
sorry, Uncle Bee.'

Uncle Bee just laughs,
and shakes his head.

'But if Grandma thought Ray
was my dad,' I ask,
'but younger,
from when he ran away,
why would she want to keep it a secret?'

Uncle Bee sits back, sighs.
'She didn't want to tell anyone.
Didn't want to get the authorities involved,
at the time, in case it made more trouble.
We didn't know who we could trust,
so, we decided to find him ourselves.'

'And did you?' I ask.

'That's a story for another day,'
Uncle Bee says, as he laughs
at his own memory.

And those words —
the promise in them,
like Mum's promise last night —
unwinds the last of the questions in my chest
until it is a big open space,
allowing me to breathe.

GRANDMA, BASIM AND ME

'I think we should maybe rescue Ray,'
Mum whispers.

I go to Grandma,
who is still holding him in a hug,
muttering:
'Basim, you came back.'

There's a sad look
in Uncle Bee's eyes
as if he knows
that time-travel can only go so far:
that Grandma can only come partially back to the present
before retreating again into the past.

But we can only do
what we can.

'Grandma?' I say,
touching her arm, gently,
hoping she'll release Ray.

She turns, looks at me,
and beams:
'Sweetie!'
and pulls me in close,
until Ray and I are both wrapped in her arms,
laughing slightly at each other's faces,
his glasses squished against my nose.

'Basim *and* Sweetie,'
I hear Grandma say.
'Today is the very best day.'

THE VERY BEST DAY

As Grandma holds Ray and me close,
I think about how
sometimes
her time-travelling memory can be a gift:
it allows her to have all her loved ones around her:
me, my dad in Ray, Uncle Bee, my mum,
even if the laws of time, of life
and death,
would seem to say otherwise.
And I realise that
in some ways
I kept my promise:
to find Dad, her Basim.
To bring him back.
Because somewhere,
in Grandma's time-travelling mind,
we are all alive at the same time.
We are all together
again.

40

WHAT I'VE LEARNED ABOUT TRAVELLING THROUGH TIME

THIS IS WHO I AM

At the end of term,
when I stand up in front of Mr Harkin's class
and deliver my presentation about
the VIP in my family,
I start with the questions that filled my notebook,
that set me off on this journey:
of figuring out the 'I Am' of me.
I start with my name.

WHAT I'VE LEARNED ABOUT
TRAVELLING THROUGH TIME

'Hi. I'm Nyla Elachi.
I know most of you know my name —
but you don't know that there's a story in it.
One of brave people choosing their own fates.
I think it's a family trait.

For my project, I decided to look for my dad.
He didn't have as much time with me
as other people's dads do,
but when he was here,
he loved lots of people:
he loved my grandma,
and Uncle Bee,
and my mum.

My family tell me he loved me too,
and I think I feel it — in them,
and in all the things he gave to me.

When I started my project,
I was looking at the space my dad left,
and I found instead all the other people
around it who help make me, me.

Researching my dad felt a bit like time-travel,
like what my grandma's memory does,
but I've learned a lot.

I've learned that it can be hard to navigate
through the sounds of people's voices,
and so the important thing is to try and hear your own.
My friends Ray, and Jess, and Miss Haldi,
taught me that.

I've learned that looking into the past
isn't just about understanding what's happened before;
it's about deciding how to go ahead.
That's something my mum knows
more than anyone.

And that history —
it can be full of questions.
Of things that hurt,
but that we can still try
to be the people who make
the world a better place.
Uncle Bee taught me that,
he's my grandma's love.
And my grandma, she
taught me that there are some things
that exist outside time —
that nothing can change,
like hugs,
or favourite days.

I've learned to follow my own two feet,
listen to myself
and, one step at a time,
I'll get where I need to go.

Even though on my adventure,
there were times when I got lost,
I think if I hadn't done,
then I wouldn't be where I am now.
Now, I know exactly where to look
to help find my way:
at my own compass.
That's what I found,
when I went looking for my dad.

I learned how to be myself.
How to say who I am.'

AFTER CLASS

Mr Harkin comes up to me.
I feel nervous about what he's about to say.

'I know I didn't stick to the assignment exactly—'
I begin,
and Mr Harkin waves my concern away,
the biggest grin on his face.

'You were grand, Nyla. GRAND.
You did exactly what I asked,
and more:
you told me about you
by telling me about your family.
You're lucky to have so many people
to call yours.'

My chest feels lighter.
I couldn't agree more.

Jess comes up
and gives me a high five,
whispering:
'Take that, Mr Davis —
greatness even with the lateness!'

I high-five her back:
'It's our family's way!'
I say, thinking about Grandma,
and Uncle Bee,
and how, despite everything,
they found each other.

I don't know how much time
they'll have together now.
I can't give them more,
or change the past.

But Ray and I,
we brought them back.

And I know that they will make the most
of each
and every
day.

AFTER SCHOOL

I rush home so fast,
I don't even have time to go to the library.
It's okay, though —
I'll see Ray and Miss Haldi later.

When I get home,
Maria looks up from Grandma's chair,
and waves hello.

Thanks to money from Uncle Bee's Forget-Me-Not Garden Fund,
we paid for Grandma's home care for six months,
which gave Mum the extra time, from not working so much,
to finally apply for a job she really wanted.
We found out that she got it,
on the same day we got support
to help fund Grandma's care, too —
and alongside Mum's new salary,
it's enough to pay for home care for Grandma.
She still visits the day care a few times a week,
to dance with her day-care friends,
but it means she won't have to move there full time.
It means she's still here when Maria,
or Mum, or I tuck her in at night.

I still try, sometimes, to convince Mum
to use up Dad's Adventure Fund,
but Mum insists on keeping her promise.

'Are you excited for tonight?'
Maria asks, her hair dyed purple this time.
I wonder what nickname Grandma will come up with for it.

I chuck my school bag on the floor,
and run over to kiss Grandma's cheek.

'I can't wait,' I say, grinning,
and I mean it.

WE'RE ON OUR WAY

That night,
Uncle Bee borrows a seven-seater minibus
from one of the musicians he knows
at The Bee Hive,
where he's been teaching me and Ray
all about music, and life,
and injustice.
About shovels,
and stories.

We all pile in:
Me, Mum, Grandma,
Miss Haldi and Ray
(whose arm has healed now,
which means we can race each other
when we go swimming together,
and shove roti canai in our mouths
at the Aunties Who Read events).

'Now, how do I work this bloomin' thing,'
Uncle Bee says, as he fiddles with the gear stick,
and Mum and him argue
(again)
over who should drive,
while me and Ray laugh,
and Grandma starts to sing,
in preparation for the ride:

'Dooo be de
doo doo doo!'

'That's right, Ruby!'
Uncle Bee shouts back,
as the engine revs,
and we all sing together
an up and down, made-up tune,
that was started by Uncle Bee
and Grandma
but is finished
by all of us.

As we set off
I notice, peeking out of the corner
of Grandma's red coat,
the edges of several open letters,
finally delivered.

I smile and look to Ray,
knowing that some friends are family,
and that we'll be both
for life.

MISS HALDI WAS RIGHT

As we walk into the school,
I think about how strange it is
seeing it at night.
I recognise a familiar scowl:
Harry.
He's standing next to his parents:
his dad in a suit,
his mum in a dress,
talking in a corner
that Mum says is for the school governors.
Both have their backs to him.
Suddenly his scowl seems less scary
and more ... unhappy.

He hasn't bothered me since
Miss Haldi's talking-to,
and since she spoke to the school.
Looking at him now,
I think about how maybe
he came for my sanctuary
because he doesn't have one of his own.

And while it doesn't change
what he said to me,
it's like seeing a bigger picture
of who he is.

I see Harry see me,
and I know what I would have done before:
lower my gaze,
try to run away.

But I don't want to do that
any more.
I want to be like Miss Haldi:
kind, but not afraid,
and always willing to fight for what's right
(one library book at a time).

I lift my head up
and meet his gaze
until he is the one
to look away.

And then I walk down the school hall,
to where my family waits.

WHEN THE CURTAINS OPEN

The whole audience goes into a hush.
We are sat on the front row.

Jess said she wanted it that way,
and bang in the middle are her parents.
I send them a wave,
and her mum blows me a giant kiss,
which Grandma pretends to catch,
and rubs it against my cheek.

The spot-light shines brightly on the stage,
and Jess steps out into the middle of it,
her pink dress sparkling,
resplendent.

I had doubted her, at first:
couldn't match sparkly sequins
with any Shakespeare play.

But as she begins to deliver her lines,
she carries us all away.

JESS WAS TELLING THE TRUTH ALL ALONG

She's good.
She's really,
really
good.

WHEN THE CURTAINS FALL

When the curtains fall,
the audience applauds
(and Jess's dad stands up
and starts whistling with his fingers,
shouting: 'Encore! Encore!')

I turn to look at my family around me:

Mum, eyes wide,
face glowing,

Miss Haldi,
clapping along,
shaking a lock of long hair
out of her eyes.

And Ray,
who nudges me,
and points further along:

at Uncle Bee and Grandma,
her head on his shoulder,
his on top of hers,

both fast
asleep.

I smile.
Stand up,
and clap and cheer
for my friend.

41

A HEARTBEAT COMPASS

STAGE DOOR FOR THE STAR

We all crowd at the side of the stage,
Miss Haldi announcing how 'Jess's interpretation
of the Shakespearean themes was
a real *bildungsroman* on stage'
— whatever that means —
and Mum passing me a bunch of flowers
to give to Jess,
ones I picked in
the Forget-Me-Not garden with Uncle Bee.

As Jess steps out,
I thrust them towards her,
and we all applaud as she bows.

We walk out together,
a big, loud bunch.

There's a woman waiting by the entrance,
wearing hospital scrubs and bright pink lipstick,
carrying a worn backpack in her hand.
Her face looks so familiar —

'Sister Amina!' I exclaim,
and turn to Ray.

We both look up at my mum,
and there're tears shining on her face,
as she runs,
and holds Amina in a hug:

'It's been so long. I've missed you.'

'I know. I've missed you, too.'

MY EVER-GROWING FAMILY

Amina smiles at me,
'I believe we spoke on the phone?'
she says. 'I'm sorry, for how I was.
Hearing Basim's name again, all the memories —
it was a lot.'

I shake my head, as if dreaming.
'I can't believe you're actually here!
How did you know it was me?'

Amina's eyes dance to Ray standing
next to me. 'I had a little help.'

I look at Ray. My wonderful friend.

Amina turns to Mum,
then back to me, her voice the same
as I heard on the phone.
'I'm sorry we lost touch.
When Basim died —
I was there that night.
He was my best friend,
and I couldn't save him.
The only way I could cope with it was to keep working,
and by the time I realised how much I'd lost,
and that I wanted to keep you guys in my life,
it felt too late — like I'd left it too long.'

One life can cause so many ripples, I think.
Not just of sadness, though. Of love.

Mum wraps her arm around Amina's shoulders.
'It's never too late,' she says.

Amina hugs Mum back,
and then turns to me,
her dark eyes sincere and shining.

'Your dad was family to me,' she says.
'We met on my first ever night shift,
and were best friends from then on —
he was my best man when my wife and I got married,
he was our kids' *favourite* uncle,
he was someone who I knew if I called him,
he'd be there.'

Sister Amina's smile wobbles,
but she carries on,
as if speaking these words means so much to her —
as if they are a story she needs to tell.
'I wanted you to know that, Nyla.
That's what I wish I'd been able to say on the call.
That your dad was' —
the word comes out in a near-whisper
as she repeats it,
filled with all the emotion of truth —
'family.'

I rush towards her,
wrapping her in a hug so tight
that I can feel her smile against my cheek.

I hope she can feel mine, too.

SISTER AMINA'S GIFT

Tears in her eyes,
Amina pulls forward the backpack
she brought with her.

'I should have given this to you years ago.
Your dad left it in his locker at work.
It's not much — mostly med stuff,
a blood pressure monitor,
that kind of thing. But they were his
and he used them every day,
and I thought, maybe
you'd want it.'

She hands the backpack to me,
and I unzip it.
Inside is a jumble of medical equipment.

My fingers brush against some paper
sticking out of the phone pocket
at the top. I pull it out.

MINE TO KEEP

'Oh, I haven't seen that in years!' Mum says,
and everyone crowds around me —
my people, I realise,
thinking of Mr Harkin's words —
Mum and Grandma and Uncle Bee
and Ray and Amina and Jess and Miss Haldi,
to stare at a Polaroid picture in my hand,
of a baby with pale brown skin
and dark curly hair
sat on her mum and dad's lap
with a stethoscope around her neck,
and him looking down at her,
proud.

'You took that,' Mum says to Grandma,
who beams with pride,
looking from Mum, to Amina, to me,
tapping the picture,
proclaiming:

'My Sweeties!'

'You must have barely been eighteen months,'
Mum says, and I turn the picture around
and see written on the back
in a new handwriting,
the one I'd been searching for all along:

'My Family.'

THIS TIME-TRAVELLER FINDS HER PLACE

I take the stethoscope out of the bag,
the same one I wore when I was a baby in the picture,
small in my mum and dad's arms.
This picture — his writing — it's mine.
Mine to keep.

I put the stethoscope to my own heart,
and listen.

It says:
alive.

I think about how my dad
must have heard this sound so many times before.

And how he'd want me to do
everything I wanted to with it.

He'd want it to adventure
and dance
and live happy
and tell stories
just like in Uncle Bee's sayings.

I close my eyes,
and listen,
making three promises
with each beat:

One, to live my life as much as I can,
whether it's going on adventures,
or holding Grandma's hand.

Two, to look out for the people around me,
and let them look out for me, too.
To cherish our stories, and
to know I can choose my own home, my own family.

Three, to realise that I'm exactly where I need to be
on my own time journey.
To realise that I'm good
exactly as,
and who,
I am.

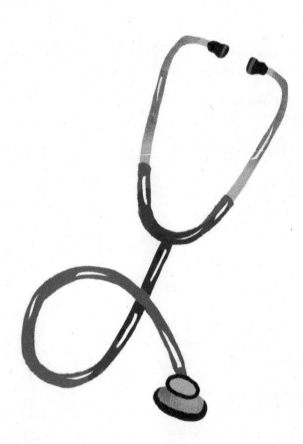

Epilogue

We climb out of the car,
Ray and I rushing towards the beach,
as Mum and Uncle Bee
wrangle with bags and beach chairs.
Grandma watches on,
clapping whenever they get something out of the boot.

'I can't believe we're doing it,
I can't believe we're actually going to swim in the sea!'
Ray says. The smile on his face
makes mine wider than I thought it could go.

'It's on the Adventure List, remember,'
I reply. 'We said we were going to — so here we are!'

Ray jumps up and down in a circle,
giddy,
around me.
Today, we're doing one of his wishes.

We started the Adventure List
before the summer holidays began,
a way for us all to honour Dad,
by adding things each of us wanted to do —
a real adventure —
and then promising we would all go on it.

It's filled with wishes big and small:
like Uncle Bee's to take us to Jamaica one day —
'we'll eat the best food you've ever tasted,
we'll have the time of our lives!' —

and Grandma's to teach us all to dance
to the tune of Uncle Bee's saxophone.
Mum's: to find a way to really have
a month of Sundays.

'You haven't written yours down yet, Nyla,'
Mum said to me as we got in the car,
and set off on our journey.
'I'm still thinking,' I said,
but I reckon Mum knows as much as I do
that for me, all of the adventures together
are a wish granted.

'Raymond!' Uncle Bee shouts,
striding on to the beach in his shorts,
with a nod to the lifeguard,
as if comparing which of them
will be better suited to save the day.
'Be careful now! I bet you the water
will be freezing!'

But Ray just grabs his hand
as he jumps into the water,
both of them squealing:
'It's so cold!' and Ray screaming —
'Uncle Bee, this is the best thing I've *ever* done!'
and Bee shouting —
'Just because I'll only go up to my knees,
doesn't mean I can't splash you, Raymond!' —
with joy.

I can hear Mum laughing,
as she throws herself down on to a beach chair
next to Grandma.
'I've got some of Uncle Bee's homegrown strawberries
and a new library book with my name on it,'
she says, and breathes out a huge sigh
as she picks up both.

I look at Grandma,
her woollen red coat
swapped for a summer shawl,
that glitters with small beads
like rubies
all along the edge.

'Shall we go and put our feet in?' I say.

She leans forward,
whispering in a conspiratorial tone:
'Let's!'

We walk towards the sea,
and the sand under my toes feels gritty,
and nice.
Grandma sighs next to me.
I know she feels it too.

When we get to the water's edge,
soft blue waves lapping over our toes,
the seagulls loud in our ears,
and Ray and Uncle Bee's laughter louder,
and Mum's relaxation,
and my smile —
all of it is as soft as a song
made by someone you love.

Grandma breathes in deeply,
as if inhaling it all,
then exclaims with delight:
'Oh, Sweetie!
Have you ever felt anything so lovely?'

'I haven't,' I say,
as I hold on to the warmth
of Grandma's palm.

Grandma leans close,
and she looks at me,
really looks at me,
her eyes clear in mine.
'Let's keep it in the most special place,'
she says, and she taps her chest,
right over where she used to keep
the photograph of Uncle Bee.

'But what if we forget?' I ask.

Grandma chuckles softly.
'Oh, Sweetie. A feeling like this
is more powerful than memory.
It stays with you forever.'
Grandma leans forward,
and taps over my heart slowly,
each word matching a beat:
'Right here.'

I squeeze her hand gently,
and she pulls me close,
before winking,
in her cheeky Grandma way,
and then we're splashing our feet
up and down in the water,
doing our own sea dance,
and Ray, Mum and Uncle Bee,
watching us, let out a cheer.
Even the lifeguard
cracks a smile.

And just like Grandma said,
with every movement —
the swirls we make in the water,
and in each other's lives,
and with every moment,
Grandma's laugh joining with mine —
we create something bigger
than memories,
something which can outlast time.
Something that will stay with us
forever.

For always.

ACKNOWLEDGEMENTS

Thank you to this book's first reader and champion, Sophie Anderson. You have been so instrumental in my journey as a children's author, and I am so grateful for your friendship, mentorship, and support through this adventure. You make the world a better place.

To my agent Gemma Cooper — how glad I am to have you in my corner! I've learned so much about being a writer from working with you, and feel like I'm in the most professional and skilled hands. Thank you for helping make a dream come true, for your advocacy and guidance, and for being brilliant at what you do.

My thanks to the team at Hachette Children's Group. To my editor Polly Lyall Grant, I love your magic mind, and that you saw this book's world through the same metaphors and images as me — like Grandma's red coat, and all it could mean. Thank you for your passion, your patience and your innovation. Thank you to everyone who has worked on and helped this book, I know there's so many more people than I know. Thank you to Ruth Girmatsion and Belinda Jones for copy-editing it so attentively, and thank you to Beth McWilliams (marketing), Binita Naik (audio), Joey Esdelle (production), Katherine Fox (sales), Annabelle El-Karim (rights), Jemimah James (international sales) and Becca Allen for her brilliant proofread. Thank you to Emily Thomas (PR), I'm so excited for all the places we'll take Nyla to! My thanks to Annabelle Steele for your brilliant authenticity read. Thank you to Jen Alliston for your beautiful design work, it means so much to me. Thank you to Sandhya Prabhat for your beautiful illustrations and your care and attention working with photographs of my family to help capture Nyla's. I can't say in words how special it is, nor how powerful.

Thank you to the team at Jonathan Ball in South Africa, with a warm shout out to Mieke Gottsche and Jean-Marie Korff, and particular thanks to Verushka Louw who made my time in Cape Town pre-release so special. Thank you Verushka for the book cover muffins, your warm welcome, our day together and everything you arranged, all of it meant so much to me. Thank you to the wonderful booksellers from Exclusive Books Cavendish and Canal Walk, Bargain Books Pinelands and Paddocks, and The Book Lounge for your enthusiasm, your welcome and company, and your eagerness to read Nyla and Grandma's story. Thank you to staff and students at St George's Grammar Cape Town for hosting the most wonderful visit, it meant so much to me to share stories with you. Thank you to librarian Elsa Goncalves for your passion for books and love of your young readers.

In order to write Nyla's identity, I had to figure out how to navigate my own on the page. I'm so grateful to the friends and loved ones who held space for me as I did. Thank you to Uncle Ebrahim for reading the sections on Zimbabwe, to Deirdre Prins-Solani for letting me run my phrasing past you, to Carmen Thompson for your read through and the conversation I needed so much. Thank you to Mustafa, for the many hours spent helping me talk this over, and for being one of the book's earliest readers and one of my biggest champions.

Thank you to Shehrezade for answering my maths questions, to Anna for your consultation on Northern Irish names, to Auntie Khutch for helping inspire Grandma Beans and for being one of the great loves of my life, to Za for consultation on the spelling of my (and Ray's!) fave, roti canai. Thank you to Ellen for answering my questions about library fire alarms, and Myra for encouraging me to see myself as I drafted my many author bios.

Thank you to Uncle Guy, for teaching me found family at a very early age. Thank you to FJ, for imprinting the value of storytelling, especially in the context of diaspora, identity and grief. Thank you to Mum for reading the manuscript with attention to Alzheimer's and Nyla's mum, and for so much more. I hope you know that our stories — of women like you, and Grandma, and me — all matter. Thank you to Ma and Aunt, for being the queens of my childhood stories.

My hugest thanks to all who have supported my career so far, from readers and workshop participants, to fellow writers who have championed me and my work, and organisations who have supported my journey. There are too many to name, but particular thanks go to the Scottish Book Trust, The Edinburgh International Book Festival, the National Library of Scotland, 404 Ink, and the Society of Authors. I'd like to thank the many brilliant booksellers, librarians and teachers who have championed my work, especially Edinburgh's Lighthouse Bookshop and Portobello Books, as well as my local community libraries past and present — you are the dearest treasures! Community is incredibly important to me, and I'd like to thank everyone who makes up mine, with particular love to everyone at Readers of Colour, as well as Rachel Sermanni, Jazmin Hundal, Nasim Rebecca Asl, Andrés N. Ordorica, Maisie Chan, Nikita Gill, Chitra Ramaswamy, Team Moniack Mhor International Writers' Residency, and so many more. Thank you to Lesa and Carmen for jumping and shouting with joy, in the middle of the street, when I told you the news. Thank you to Dean Atta — who planted the idea that I should try to write in verse. Thank you to my dearest friends Heather and Johanna.

Thank you to the people who — like Miss Haldi says — take all of their brave and choose to make a difference. The people who grow stories like trees which provide a space for others to rest under. Thank you to those who paved the way. And, to all the kids who, like me, never found stories that spoke to all the questions inside them — this book is for you, too.

Thank you to Dani, who loved a good book, and who wanted us all to live our lives fully and do the things we want to do with them. Thank you to Grandma, for the promise you insisted I make to you again and again in your time-traveller way. Every time I keep my promise to you, I realise that it is in fact a gift from you to me, and one that lives beyond the constraints of time.

To the one I want to tell all my stories to, and the one whose stories I always want to listen to: Mustafa. Thank you for the foundation of happiness and love and acceptance that you create in my life, which allowed me to be brave enough and free enough to write this book. I love you. I am proud of you. You are the love of my life.

I remember telling my grandma that I'd written a poem about her, once, when she was having a difficult time-travel day. 'Oh!' she said, 'That's made the sun come out, that has.' I hope this book makes the sun come out, for so many people. I hope, in readers' hands and hearts, it makes it shine.